T0090140

Mistakes
Men Make

Also by Byron Harmon

All the Women I've Loved

Published by Pocket Books

Mistakes
Men Make

BYRON HARMON

POCKET BOOKS
New York   London   Toronto   Sydney

POCKET BOOKS, a division of Simon & Schuster, Inc.
1230 Avenue of the Americas, New York, NY 10020

This book is a work of fiction. Names, characters, places and incidents are products of the author's imagination or are used fictitiously. Any resemblance to actual events or locales or persons, living or dead, is entirely coincidental.

Copyright © 2005 by Byron Harmon

All rights reserved, including the right to reproduce
this book or portions thereof in any form whatsoever.
For information address Pocket Books, 1230 Avenue
of the Americas, New York, NY 10020

Library of Congress Cataloging-in-Publication Data

Harmon, Byron.
   Mistakes men make / by Byron Harmon.—1st Pocket Books trade
pbk. ed.
      p. cm.
   ISBN-13: 978-0-7434-8309-4
   ISBN-10:   0-7434-8309-X
      1. Television news anchors—Fiction. 2. Self-destructive behavior—
Fiction. 3. Loss (Psychology)—Fiction. 4. New York (N.Y.)—Fiction.
I. Title.

PS3608.A748M57 2005
813'.6—dc22

                                                            2005045814

First Pocket Books trade paperback edition July 2005

10 9 8 7 6 5 4 3 2 1

POCKET and colophon are registered trademarks of
Simon & Schuster, Inc.

Manufactured in the United States of America

For information regarding special discounts for bulk purchases,
please contact Simon & Schuster Special Sales at 1-800-456-6798
or business@simonandschuster.com

I dedicate this book to my father, David Harmon.
I love you, Pops.

Acknowledgments

There are so many people who have been instrumental in my success, not only as an author and executive producer but also as a human being. It would take volumes just to thank them all. However, there are a few who I have almost daily contact with who I affectionately call my circle. They are my mother, Shirley, my brothers, Marshall and Andre, and his wife, Carla. My girlfriend, Rhadia Hursey, and her family. My brothers from another mother: Doug Bennett, Eric Devillar, Gregory Blue, and Michael Wilson. My Ill Relatives, Marcus, Ryal, and DrakMuse. My own review team, sisters Kay and Kelly. My longtime friends Jennifer Wiggins, Corrin Johnson, and Lauren Petterson. The talented Shon Gables and my right-hand man, Shannon Lanier.

I want to thank Louise Burke and Simon & Schuster for giving me a chance to share my artistry. I also want to thank Louise Burke for assigning Selena James, an editor of immense talent, to work with me. Selena, you have been a wonderful source of strength and friendship. I owe so much to you.

I want to thank my agents, Tracy Sherrod and Lane Zachary. I want to thank Carol Mackey at Black Expressions. And I can't forget my girls Kimberly Hines and Tia Shabazz at Pentouch.com. It all started with you. Thanks.

Chapter One

Eric Swift had always dreamed of making love to Janet Jackson, and tonight his dream was about to come true. Ever since he'd moved from Washington, D.C., to New York to take a top anchoring job at ABC eight months before, he'd had one conquest after another. On the career front, it was clear to everyone he worked with that his star was on the rise. As the sports anchor for an early morning show he brought an exciting spin to sports reporting. Most days his schedule allowed him to get off work by noon. That left him with plenty of free time, and so far he'd made the most of it—with the ladies. He'd been out with nearly a dozen different women, but this was the first time he'd bought a brand-new outfit for a date. That's if you wanted to call it a date. Actually, they were going to have dinner and drinks in her suite at the posh W Hotel on Lexington Avenue in Manhattan. Janet had said she was tired and not up for the crowds of people who would definitely be out on such a hot Friday evening in May. Eric had tried, without success, to convince her to come to his apartment at Trump Place, a new luxury development on the Upper West Side.

As he slid his toned arms inside the beige linen three-button Prada suit jacket, Eric smiled at the way the light set off the silk mustard yellow shirt. He left the two top buttons undone to showcase his muscular neck and strong jaw. The tailored suit fit him like a glove, but he frowned at his footwear.

No, no, he thought. *These are just too old.*

He strolled over to the walk-in closet of his impressive master bedroom. He'd had his decorator copy a room that he'd seen showcased in *Architectural Digest*. It was an exact replica, from the mini crystal chandelier to the thick mocha-colored carpet.

Despite being a playboy and former NFL cornerback, Eric was no dumb jock. He was very well read and had a particular fondness for ancient cultures and history. The decor was Old World Spanish with a dash of Middle East. His king-sized antique bed with matching nightstands was at least one hundred years old. The bedroom set was made of heavy oak and Pledged to perfection. The thick maroon and brown Ralph Lauren duvet and pillows matched the heavy silk curtains. The bedroom looked like an expensive Moroccan hotel room.

Gracing the brass lamp-lit walls were tasteful prints by prominent African American artists. The prints, as well as the African and Arabic sculptures nestled in custom-built oak bookshelves, were his prized possessions. Among them, the sculpture closest to his heart was a wooden Black Madonna and child from Ethiopia. It had once been part of an altar in one of the oldest Coptic churches in Addis Ababa. Eric had to jump through major customs hoops to get it out of the country.

Switching on the overhead light in the closet, he scanned the neat boxes of shoes until his gaze rested on the perfect pair. "Yes, these babies will do," he said.

Eric was a freak for shoes, but not just any shoes. He only wore Mezlans, an expensive brand imported from Spain. He carefully slipped on a brand-new brown pair along with a matching belt.

Impressed with his reflection, he said "Goddamn!" to the mirror hanging inside one of the double doors of the closet.

Eric couldn't believe how lucky he was. Who knew that his friend Dre would know a woman as fly as Janet Jackson? Kenneth Andre, aka Dirty Dre or Stuttering Dre, wasn't known for his taste in pretty women. Not that he didn't have any women. In fact, Dirty Dre was quite a player. It's just that his team wore ugly uniforms. "Ugly women need d-d-dick too" was his motto. It didn't matter if the club or party was full of dozens of blind, naked, and horny Tyra Banks look-alikes, Dirty Dre would somehow manage to leave with the Bride of Frankenstein. That's why Eric had demanded proof of Janet's beauty when Dre told him about her a month ago. He wanted to see for himself if she looked as fine as the real Janet Jackson.

"N-n-n-nigga, you want proof?" Dirty Dre had said, reaching into his back pocket for his wallet. "Here's your proof."

Eric held the photograph up to the light and studied it. He was impressed. Too impressed.

"This picture came with your wallet," he cracked.

Dirty Dre frowned.

"Well, I'll be damned, Dirty. How did you meet her?"

"She go way b-b-back with my sister. They um, did like ballet or some sh-sh-shit together when they were little girls."

"Well, Janet Jackson ain't no little girl no mo," Eric said, his hand on his crotch. "She looks old enough to 'control' this. You didn't hit it, huh, Dirty?"

"H-hell no," he shot back. "She too damn pretty."

If Janet lived up to her picture, he thought he might have to settle down. He'd called Janet later that week and they hit it off great. She was funny, charming, and above all, sounded fine as hell on the phone. He couldn't wait to hook up with her. Pops, Eric's father and confidant, was even excited and had told him to call after they hooked up to give him the play-by-play.

Early-evening traffic in Manhattan was always crazy, and Eric arrived at the W Hotel about twenty minutes late. *Fuck it*, he thought. *I'm late, but I'm fashionably late. Plus I'm fly as hell.*

He started humming the chorus to Michael Jackson's "Beat It" as he pushed the elevator button. That's exactly what he planned to do to Janet. He couldn't believe how nasty she'd talked on the phone. By the time he knocked on Janet's hotel door, his heart was racing with excitement.

"Just a minute," Janet said through the door.

"Oh, it's gon' be more than just a minute," Eric muttered to himself. With a smirk he stuck his right hand in his pants pocket and cocked his chin a few degrees to the left, his most Mac-a-licious pose. The door swung open and there stood Janet Jackson in all her glory. Eric thought he heard trumpets blaring and angels singing. She had on a sexy form-fitting white dress with a V-neck that ended at her navel. Her right foot, barely peeking out from under the dress, was balanced in a three-inch-heeled pink and white Jimmy Choo sandal, which matched the pink flower in her long black hair. On her neck and wrist was a matching platinum diamond necklace and bracelet set. It was hard for Eric to believe, but she looked even better than her picture.

Eric had planned to say some smooth shit, but all he could spit out was "Damn!"

Janet's laugh was high and sweet. "Is that all you got to say, Eric?"

"If I say what I'm thinking, you might call hotel security," he said, shaking his head.

Janet smirked. "Go ahead. I'm sure I've heard it before."

Eric got down on one knee. "Will you marry me?"

"What? Boy, you are even crazier than Dre said."

"Look, I know a preacher who makes booty calls, I mean house calls. I got his two-way number and I can get him here right now."

"Your pastor has a two-way? Wait a second, what would we do for a ring?"

Standing up, he twisted the ring off his finger. "You can wear this."

"That's a graduation ring."

"It's solid gold."

"Boy, come in here."

"I plan to."

Janet grinned and turned around slowly. Eric's gaze followed her shapely ass as if he was watching a scene in digital slow motion, one cheek after the other. As she walked farther into the room, Eric blinked and rubbed his eyes. Then he blinked again.

"What the fuck?" he mumbled.

Janet was limping. Not a simple sprained-ankle limp but a full-blown she-must-have-had-polio-as-a-little-girl limp.

She looked over her shoulder. "Don't be scared. Walk this way."

"I can't walk that way," Eric said, dazed and confused.

Janet looked surprised. "What's wrong? Didn't Dre tell you?"

"Tell me what?"

"That I had a prosthetic leg."

Still standing in the doorway, Eric swallowed hard, eyes bugging. "You got only one leg?"

"Yeah, I had a traffic accident about five years ago and they had to amputate my left leg."

"Huh?" Eric stuttered. "You left your leg? I mean, you lost your left leg?"

"I can't believe Andre didn't tell you."

"Mother-fuck!" Eric said, shaking his head.

"What did you say?"

"Oh. Um, I said you had some tough luck."

"It's okay. At least I'm alive."

Eric looked at his watch. "Yeah, that's one way of looking at it."

"So what now? You don't wanna come in?"

"Oh yeah, I'm cool." *Okay, how do I get out of this?*

Eric closed the door behind him and leaned back against it. It sounded like a cell door clanking on death row. He tugged at his shirt collar and cleared his throat. "You have anything to drink in here? I'm feeling a lil' parched."

"Yeah, I ordered a nice bottle of wine."

"What kind?"

"A Merlot."

Eric frowned.

"You don't like Merlot? I can order something else. What would you like?"

"Some Mad Dog twenty-twenty."

It was the drink of choice for what he imagined would be an Olympian sex effort. No, it was worse than that. . . . Tonight was shaping up to be a Special Olympics.

Chapter Two

"Please don't tell me you hit it," LeBaron Brown whispered into the phone. He was Eric's best friend from his days working at FOX in D.C. LeBaron, who was also a newly-wed, cautiously looked over his shoulder to see if Phoenix, his wife in the next room, was listening.

"Did I hit it?" Eric laughed. "Not only did I hit it, I damn near ripped off her fake-ass leg. It's been two days since we hooked up and I'm still sore."

Eric was on his cell phone downstairs at Le Bar Bat, a trendy Manhattan bar on West Fifty-seventh Street. It was the First Friday party at the club, and even though it was only 6 PM, the club was starting to fill up.

"You are out of control," LeBaron howled.

"Her legs were out of control. And get this? She wanted me to talk dirty to her."

LeBaron was shaking with laughter. "What did you say?"

Eric looked around grinning, then cupped his hand over the cell phone. "I was like, 'Take it with ya' one-legged ass.' "

LeBaron laughed so hard he started snorting.

"I tried to hit it from the back and she fell off the bed. I'm standing there with my Johnson in one hand and her leg in the other."

"You a fool." LeBaron tried to catch his breath. "You tell Pops?"

"You know I did."

"What did he say?"

"What does Pops always say?"

"Your ass needs to settle down?"

"Bingo."

"Hold on a second, Eric. I got something wild to tell you."

"You had sex with a girl in a wheelchair?"

"No, fool. Phoenix is pregnant."

"Phoenix is what?" Eric said, nearly spitting out his Heineken.

"That's right, dog," LeBaron said, a smile on his face. "My ass is 'bout to be a daddy."

"Yo' ass is 'bout to be broke," Eric laughed, curling his lips into a disapproving frown. "How many months?"

"Three."

"Three months!" Eric straightened up on the bar stool.

"But damn, ya'll ain't been married but a month. Who the daddy?" They both laughed.

"You know we've been married for nearly six months."

Eric raised his bottle and said loudly, "Well, I guess congratulations are in order, Big Papa." Two people at the other end of the bar frowned. Eric frowned back.

"Whoa, try and contain your enthusiasm," LeBaron said.

"Oh, c'mon, bruh. You know I'm happy for you. It's just . . ." Eric mumbled, staring at his beer.

"Just what?" LeBaron demanded.

"You're getting soft. Why do you want to have some damn kids? Running around tearing shit up. I bet Phoenix got your ass wearing briefs."

"What!" LeBaron said in disbelief. "That may be the dumbest shit you've ever said, and you've said some incredibly dumb shit."

"You know how I am."

"Yeah, petty."

"Whatever. First you get married, now you're having a baby. I mean, damn. We're the same age and shit. You making a nigga feel old."

"You damn sho' don't act old."

"What's that supposed to mean?"

"Forget it, man."

"Yeah, later for that shit. We supposed to be celebrating." Eric waved the attractive bartender over. She could have been actress Gabrielle Union's younger sister.

"Listen to this, LeBaron," he said, holding the phone to the bartender's ear. "Hey, miss, can I get another round? My boy here on the phone is going to be a baby daddy. Tell him hi."

"Congratulations," she said into the phone. "The drink is on the house."

"Well, if it's free, I'll take a bottle of Cristal," Eric cracked.

The bartender gave him a Negro, please look.

"Okay," Eric grinned, bringing the cell phone back to his ear. "Make that a Heineken." The bartender was so cute Eric couldn't resist flirting. "Oh my God, you have a beautiful smile," he said, a devious grin forming on his face. "I bet when you smile, the sun gets jealous."

"Boy, you are crazy," she gushed. Her teeth were as white as Michael Jackson wanted to be. "But thank you. Your smile is quite nice too."

"Thanks. I'm a dentist." Eric grinned.

"Really?" she asked.

"No," he laughed. "But you know something? You look familiar."

"Really?"

"Yeah, you look like my first wife."

"You were married?" she said, arching her right eyebrow.

"Not yet." Eric deadpanned.

On the other end of the phone, LeBaron nearly fell out of his easy chair laughing. He'd heard Eric use that line a thousand times and it killed him every time. The bartender didn't get it and walked off with a confused look on her face.

"You're still the same ol' Eric," LeBaron said. "Anyway, bruh, how is the Big Apple treating you?"

"I'll tell you something, LeBaron. I thought that moving here and taking the sports anchor gig was going to be a tough transition, but I love it. I am in my element."

"We all miss you. It's not the same without you here at FOX. How long has it been?"

"Eight months."

"It's been that long?"

"Yeah. I miss you guys too, but you know, everybody has to move on. You're on a whole other level with Phoenix now. You don't need me there to be fucking up a good thing."

"Ain't that the truth? By the way, how's ABC? I heard they work a brother like a slave and—"

Eric cut him off. "What TV station doesn't? But for six hundred and fifty thousand dollars a year, I'll pick cotton on live TV eating a piece of corn bread."

"Damn." LeBaron laughed. "That's what they're paying you?"

"In large bills. But that's only a quarter of what they pay the network football analysts."

"You still got your sights set on that, huh?"

"That's the main reason I moved here. I'm going all the way to the top with this."

"All work and no *play*? That doesn't sound like the Eric I know."

Eric waved the bartender over for another beer. "Oh, there is plenty of play for the playa. In fact, wait until I send you a tape of one of my coanchors. Oh, my God."

LeBaron cut him off. "What's her name?"

"The ass on her."

"Eric, what's her name?"

"Her ass leaves me shocked and awed."

LeBaron laughed. "What's her name?"

"Oh, Eden."

"Eden. As in the Garden of Eden?"

"Yeah, Eden Alexander. Isn't that a great name?"

"She cute?"

"Is she cute? Nigga, *Webster's* hasn't invented the word to describe what she is."

"Damn, she's like that?"

"She *is* like that. Yo, the first time I met her was my first day on the air. I had seen tapes of her, but to see her in person? LeBaron, I almost couldn't read the teleprompter."

"Damn, hurry up and send *me* a tape."

Eric looked around, then lowered his voice to a whisper. "And you know I can't wait to get up in Eden's secret garden."

"You guys went out yet?"

"Nah, it's taken me six months just to get her to have a conversation with me. She's superfocused on her work."

"She got a man?"

"Not sure, but I know she's checking me out."

"How you know that?"

"Because she's ignoring me."

LeBaron laughed. "Well, loverboy, what's your plan?"

Eric smiled. "The three P's."

"Not the three P's." LeBaron laughed.

"Yes," Eric snickered. "Persistence, poetry, and plenty of *pimping*."

Chapter Three

For the past month, one of the hottest stories floating around New York City had been the rumor of a bombshell tell-all book by NFL Hall of Famer Lawrence Taylor. The autobiography, titled *Over the Edge: Tackling Drugs, Quarterbacks, and a World Beyond Football,* was rumored to contain a sordid story of sex, drugs, and the inside scoop of the macho world of professional football. The book wouldn't be released for another two weeks, and while every sports anchor had tried to get an advance copy, so far it was being held under tight wraps. But while the other anchors had been scrambling to get the book, Eric had landed the author himself. As the control room and floor crew listened to Eric's interview, there was an air of reverence inside the studio. After all, this was LT, the greatest linebacker in the history of the game. The entire studio crew was impressed that Eric had managed to get *the get* of the season. It was a testament to his contacts and wasn't going unnoticed by the brass at ABC Sports. Eric hoped it didn't go unnoticed by Eden either.

"LT?" Eric asked. "What I want to know, and frankly what the New York Giants fans want to know, is were you high during the games?"

"Oh no, Eric," LT said, looking him dead in the eyes. "I'd never do that. But as I said before, after the game? Now that's a different story."

"Last question, LT. Do you still get high?"

The football legend sighed. It was the sound of a man worn out by fighting demons. "No, but I ain't gonna lie, it's an everyday struggle."

Eric reached over and shook his hand. "Thanks for your time."

"My pleasure. It's refreshing to talk to someone who actually played the game. Keep up the good work, Eric."

"Whoa, thanks, LT. If I had lighter skin, I'd blush." Eric laughed, then turned to the camera and said, "Tomorrow, I'll have Derek Outlaw live, the star NFL wide receiver who may be joining the New York Giants." Eric smiled at the camera as the show went to a commercial break. He shook hands with Lawrence Taylor before he was whisked away by his publicist, then walked by the anchor desk, where Eden sat. She waved him over. "That was a great interview, Eric."

"Thanks."

"You've been breaking some big stories lately. What's your secret?"

He thought for a moment. "I don't know. Call it persistence."

Eden smiled at his comment. Eric walked away, hoping his surprise didn't show on his face. He always made it a point to speak to Eden every day, but today was the first time he could remember that Eden initiated a conversation. The three P's were working faster than he'd planned.

Good Morning New York on ABC's channel 7 was fast becoming one of the hottest shows in New York City. After enduring years of finishing last place in the ratings, it was finally enjoying success. Many owed the rise in ratings to the addition of the new female anchor from Detroit, Eden Alexander. Eden was black movie star beautiful. Standing five feet six, she was track star lean. Her shoulder length bob was augmented by a near imperceptible weave that never needed tightening. She was alluring with a pinch of attitude. At least once a week she'd correct someone with a "No, Chanté Moore looks like me."

Beautiful and bubbly, Eden had the perfect traits for a morning show anchor. The *New York Daily News* had dubbed her "The Black Katie Couric." It said Eden was "as adept at making fun of herself as she was at getting a guest to cry during an interview." The usually gruff New York market took an instant liking to her. Her coanchor,

Ryan Sanchez, was known as the Hispanic Tom Brokaw because of his "just the facts" approach to news reading. Rounding out the team was the legendary crazy weatherman, Steve Rice, recently stolen from the local WB network station, and sports anchor Eric Swift. It took a lot to get New Yorkers to watch television at five-thirty in the morning, and the diverse group brought a mix of fun and edge to the normally conservative television market.

For the average person, an anchor job in the number one television market would be the capstone of a great career. But for thirty-two-year-old Eden Alexander, the morning show was just a stepping-stone. In the parlance of television, her ultimate goal was to "get to the network." She wanted national exposure and would let nothing and no one get in her way.

"And thanks for joining us this morning," Eden said as she began to wrap up another show. It was a good-bye she had said a thousand times. "I'm Even Alexander. I mean, um . . . excuse me, I'm Eden Alexander. Have a great day, New York." Beside her, Ryan grinned. Eden's smile was plastic until the commercial rolled, and then it melted into a snarl.

"Dammit! Did you hear that shit?" she yelled to no one in particular. "My name was misspelled on the prompter. People will think I can't even say my damn name right. Ugh!" She threw her earpiece onto the anchor desk and stormed toward the control room. She dodged a gauntlet of cameras and cables before pushing the door open, nearly running into Karen Cohen, her young and still somewhat green line producer. Eden composed herself by smoothing the jacket edges of her red Prada pantsuit.

"Karen?" she asked through clenched tenth. "How many times do I have to tell you about misspellings? Don't you proofread? Did you hear what just happened?" The questions were rapid and dripped with anger. Karen just stood there, her face blank. The middle-aged director and other control room personnel glanced at each other and smiled, clearly enjoying the spectacle.

Karen cleared her throat. "Well, Eden—" she began.

"No, I'll tell you what happened," Eden cut her off. "You made me look like an ass out there. And I don't like looking like an ass. So you better get it together, girl, or I'll make sure we hire somebody who will." Eden turned and bumped into Eric. He barely heard her mumble, "I'll never make it to the network working with these fools."

By the time she made it to her office and slammed the door, it felt as if a tornado had blown through the newsroom.

"Hey, Eden," Eric whispered after softly knocking on her office door. "You okay?"

"No, I'm very mad," she pouted. The irony was that her office looked so happy. All lilies and sunlight. The office smelled of Christian Dior's Addict. Framed pictures of her at various civic and professional events were neatly placed on her desk. The biggest and most ornate one framed a photo of Eden and the world's greatest female superhero, Oprah Winfrey. Eric gently pushed the door open.

"Mind if I come in?" he said with a sheepish grin.

"I don't really feel like—"

"Thanks," he cut her off, ignoring her. He plopped down in a chair in front of her desk.

Eden frowned. "I see you don't take no for an answer."

"Not when I see a damsel in distress," he said, flashing all thirty-twos.

"Oh, and you think I'm in distress?"

"Maybe not in distress, per se, but stressed nevertheless."

"Ain't that the truth? But don't come in here and tell me how I overreacted. I feel like being pissed."

"You didn't overreact."

"Come again," she said, not believing what she just heard.

"You didn't overreact. In fact, I think you were too calm. You had every right to be pissed. Here you are, an anchor in New York City, the nation's number one television market, and these Ivy League–educated green-assed white girl producers can't even spell."

"Thank you. Finally a voice of reason," she concurred.

"It's your face out there, not theirs," he continued. "Who looks like the ass?"

"Me."

"Right." *But what a beautiful ass*, he thought. "Honestly, I think you should be even more diva-ish."

"Really? Nah, I don't want that reputation. I just want people to do their jobs. I come in early. I'm involved in the segments. I research. Is it too much to ask for them to do the same?"

"I think that's reasonable," Eric agreed. "But here's how I see your situation. That is if I may be frank?"

Eden smiled. "Yes, Frank. Please tell me how you see my, um, situation."

Clearing his throat, he began. "Eden, I call it like I see it. You are a star. Obviously the brass at ABC is grooming you for the next level, which is the network. You are global, not local. Look at how the numbers have sparked since you arrived last year. You are destined for the big leagues. This morning show is nothing but a pit stop. So your focus should be on making yourself better. There is nothing wrong with that. Don't be ashamed of that. This is the number one market, and since I am the sports anchor, allow me to use a sports analogy. Eden, you are the number one pick and you deserve to be working with first string players."

"I'd have to say that I agree with you. But what do I do?"

"Exactly what you are doing." Eric leaned in closer. "After the way you honey-roasted her ass, I guarantee you Karen will quadruple-check her damn scripts from now on. Don't take shit from anyone. Remember, you're doing

ABC a favor by working here, not the other way around. Just keep demanding excellence and you will achieve it. Claim it, it's your right."

"Claim it? You sound like T. D. Jakes. Do you go to church?"

"Um, every chance I get," he lied.

Eden looked skeptical. "Did you go last Sunday?"

"I didn't get the chance," he deadpanned.

"You're crazy, but thanks for the pep talk, Eric. I feel better now." Eden looked at the clock. "Oh my goodness, I have a news cut-in in a few minutes."

They both stood, and right before they got to the door, Eden and Eric looked at each other. Simultaneously they both blurted out, "We should have lunch."

"What about Friday?" Eric said, laughing.

"Friday it is," Eden said, running toward the studio.

Eric stared at her run, as if she moved in HDTV super slow motion. *Goddamn, she got a thong on*, he thought, making eye contact with an intern eyeing him eyeing Eden.

That's one lucky thong.

Chapter Four

Eric couldn't get Eden out of his mind, not even after his daily two-hour workout. It had been three hours since their conversation in her office, and the lovely sight of her was still fresh in his thoughts. *Maybe a good book could relieve my mind of the lust*, he thought. After a very cold shower, he pondered his choices.

Eric had a wide range of literary tastes. Spread out on his coffee table next to a very tall glass of Captain Morgan rum and Coke were three books: *The Case for Faith*, a treatise on spirituality, *The Billion Dollar BET*, a book about Black Entertainment Television, and *A History of X*, which was about the porn industry. Tough choices.

"*A History of X* it is," Eric said with a devilish grin.

As he began to read through the book's X-rated introduction his phone rang. He looked at the caller ID. It was his mother, Shirley, calling from Atlanta. He had bought his parents a house down there nearly ten years ago. Eric was glad he was able to get them out of the small house in

Atlanta they'd lived in since moving from the South Bronx. He looked at his watch. It was 2 PM. Shirley rarely called him during the week.

"Hey, Ma," Eric said, connecting his earpiece. There was no such thing as a short call from Shirley.

"Some girl sent some flowers here for you," she said, sounding slightly irritated. "And they're stinking up my house."

"They're for you, Mama," he corrected her.

"Huh?" Shirley was confused. "For me. It's not my birthday. What for?"

"Just because," Eric said. He loved messing with his mother.

"Because what?"

"Because I l-o-v-e you," he sang. "Can't a son send his mama some flowers just because?"

For once Shirley was at a loss for words.

"Mama?"

"In that case, thank you, son. They're beautiful."

Eric smiled.

"Boy, you so retarded. By the way, Tayja wants to thank you for buying her new school clothes. She made you a special card."

"Really?" Eric beamed. "Tell her thanks."

"Tell her yourself, she's right here." Shirley lifted the five-year-old future beauty queen up to her knee and gave her the phone.

"Hi, Unca Eric," Tayja said, fumbling with the phone.

"Hey, baby. How's my favorite niece?"

"Fine."

"You like the clothes your uncle bought you?"

"Uh-huh." She giggled. "Momo say I'ma be the goodest looking girl in school."

Eric chuckled so hard his eyes teared. Tayja put her grandmother back on the phone.

"Lord, that girl growing like a weed." Shirley exhaled as Tayja jumped off her knee and scampered into the living room.

"Too bad Sean ain't there to see it," Eric said sarcastically.

"Don't start with that." Shirley's tone was testy. In the last few years any talk of Eric's younger brother seemed to turn any conversation ugly.

"Why not?" Eric shot back. "It's the truth."

"We all have our troubles," she said. "Even you, Mister Perfect."

"I'm not perfect."

"Well, quit acting like it. Now that you're in New York, why haven't you visited him?" she demanded. "He's been there ten months."

"Mama, I'm allergic to prison. And convicts."

"Eric, watch your mouth, you're talking about your brother."

"I know, Mama, but I can't stand to see Sean locked up. You know how close we are. I feel like it's my fault."

"Eric, your brother is a grown man. You didn't sell him those drugs."

"Okay, Mama, I'ma go see him soon. Is Pops home?"

"Yeah, but he's about to walk out the door. Hold on."

Eric could hear his mother yelling for his father, David, to come to the phone. He could also hear him grumbling.

"Hello?" Pops said in a gravelly voice.

"Where you going, old man?"

"I'm the father, remember? I don't have to tell you shit."

"Don't tell me you're going fishing again."

"So what?"

"Must be nice to be retired."

Pops laughed. "It's your fault. You knew better than to buy me a boat. Got your mama thinking I'm cheating."

"That's right, blame it on the children," Eric cracked. "Catch something for me, Pops."

"I'll try. Love you, son."

"Love you too."

Eric was about to hang up when his father said, "Eric?"

"Yeah, Pops?"

"Go visit your brother."

"I will, Pops. I promise."

Eric hung up the phone and pushed his book aside. He wasn't eager to visit Sean. Having a convict for a brother put a cramp in his style, and he didn't want anyone to find out about Sean, especially Eden. Maybe he could convince LeBaron to go with him to visit Sean. If anyone ever asked why he'd visited a prison, he could say he'd just been accompanying his good friend while he visited an inmate.

Then Eric thought about Phoenix. No way was a pregnant Phoenix going to let LeBaron go anywhere.

Chapter Five

The last six months had been eventful for LeBaron and Phoenix. They had gotten married and moved into a beautiful four-bedroom house. The house sat on one and a half acres in Mitchelleville, Maryland, a wealthy and predominantly black suburb outside Washington, D.C. Adding to the fairy-tale beginning of their marriage was Phoenix's pregnancy. It was the source of a whole lot of joy, for LeBaron, and a little pain as well.

There never seemed to be enough time in the day for LeBaron. Phoenix had taken leave from her job as a buyer for Saks Fifth Avenue, but taking a leave wasn't an option for LeBaron. He had to balance his job as an executive producer at FOX and his role as a loving husband. LeBaron was logging many miles taking Phoenix to and from the doctor. Lately, she had always seemed to be on edge. Today wasn't any different. And although it was a routine visit, Phoenix was in no mood to play.

"You okay, baby?" LeBaron asked Phoenix as she took a seat in the obstetrician's waiting room. "Need me to go out to the car and get your pillow?"

She frowned. He looked frazzled as he fussed over her. Although she was only four months pregnant, he acted as if she was on bed rest.

"LeBaron, I can sit down by myself. I'm pregnant, not helpless," Phoenix scolded him while pushing his arm away.

He patted her shoulder. "I'm sorry, baby. Just trying to get you comfortable."

"What you are *getting* is on my nerves. Dang," she said, pushing his arm away again.

He ignored her and reached into his jacket. "You want a candy bar, baby?"

"I want you to leave me alone."

LeBaron looked at a soon to be new dad sitting next to him and shrugged his shoulders. Future Dad shrugged back. LeBaron leaned over and surveyed the selection of magazines. He sighed. "Dang, all they got is women's magazines."

Phoenix stared at him hard. "What did you expect? *Guns and Ammo*?"

The soon to be new dad next to LeBaron giggled until his wife elbowed him and said, "I don't hear nothing funny."

"Baby, your hormones are acting up," LeBaron observed.

"Let's see how chummy you'd be if you felt fat as a pig and threw up every day."

He rolled his eyes. "Girl, you keep this up and we both gon' be in the hospital. You having a baby and me having a heart attack."

LeBaron loved being a husband, but the prospect of becoming a father terrified him. The responsibility of a wife plus raising a child kept him in a state of high anxiety. In the past few months he'd bought a library of books on parenthood, but they were of no help. He watched hours of talk shows and even bought a Dr. Phil DVD, but still he found no answers. He even called his mother, but what Lucille told him could land him in the state's child welfare database. He smiled just thinking about it.

"Mama, I'm scared," he'd said during a recent visit to Louisiana. "I don't know the first thing about raising a child."

"Shit, boy. There ain't but three things you need to know about raising kids."

"What's that, Mama?" he'd asked, feeling confused.

"You have to feed 'em, clothe 'em, and tear they lil' asses up when they do wrong. You got's to whip they ass. That's what me and your daddy did to you and your brother, and look how ya'll turned out."

Yeah, scared that we'd do the same thing to our kids, he thought.

"Quit daydreaming," Phoenix said, nudging his shoulder. "The nurse called my name."

"Oh, sorry." He started to help her up, but her scowl made him pull back.

The nurse took them into an examination room. After about fifteen minutes, Phoenix's doctor knocked on the door.

"Good morning," the doctor said.

"Hi, Dr. Peterson," the couple said. Phoenix really liked Dr. Gwen Peterson. She was brilliant, black, and had a great bedside manner. She was also very fly.

"Dr. Peterson, is that Gucci you have on under that lab coat?" LeBaron said flirtatiously.

Dr. Peterson smiled. "You always know just what to say, LeBaron."

"Yeah," Phoenix said, staring daggers at him. "LeBaron always knows just what to say."

LeBaron turned his head and eyed a wall chart describing diabetes' effect on the circulatory system.

Dr. Peterson cleared her throat and opened up a folder. "I have the results of your tests."

"And?" the couple said expectantly.

"I think we need to run some more tests. I think you may have preeclampsia."

"Preeclampsia?" LeBaron repeated, then turned to Phoenix. She sat silently on the examination table.

Dr. Peterson smiled. "Yes, preeclampsia or toxemia. It's a disease that can affect the brain, kidney, and liver. It's characterized by swelling, high blood pressure, and protein in the urine."

"What causes it?" Phoenix asked. "Did I do something wrong?"

LeBaron held her hand. "No, baby, I'm sure you didn't."

"LeBaron's right, Phoenix. It happens in about five to ten percent of all pregnancies. We call it the mystery disease. No one really knows what causes it."

LeBaron stroked his chin. "What's next?"

"Well," Dr. Peterson said. "Phoenix is going into her second trimester, so we caught it early."

"And that's good, right?" LeBaron asked.

"Yes, that's good, but that doesn't mean she's out of the woods."

"What does this mean? Can we lose the baby?"

Dr. Peterson cleared her throat. "Well, there is a chance of miscarriage."

Phoenix began to cry. LeBaron held her hand tighter. "What are the chances?" he asked.

Dr. Peterson shot a concerned glance at Phoenix. Her face was buried in her hands. LeBaron stood and held her.

"I'd have to say about fifty-fifty."

LeBaron closed his eyes and said a short prayer. He couldn't help but think of Eric and something he had told him at his wedding.

"There is no doubt that having a child is going to change your life," Eric had said. "The problem is you don't know if it will for the best."

Chapter Six

"This chicken panang is incredible," Eden mumbled, pointing her fork at the spicy Thai dish.

Eric, his mouth filled with a spring roll, nodded in agreement. "Tang's has some of the best Thai food in the city."

Zagat's Restaurant Guide had recently given the hot new Asian eatery its highest rating. Located on Fifty-ninth street between Fifth and Madison Avenue, the place was always packed and a reservation was a must. Unless, of course, you were tight with Salleen, the maître d'—Eric was. A pair of Jets tickets on the fifty-yard line was all it took to secure VIP treatment.

Eric and Eden were seated in a plush leather booth in the back. The area was dimly lit. Miles Davis was playing softly in the background. Eric was hoping that by the end of their lunch he'd know Eden a little better.

"That's a wonderful outfit you have on," Eric said, admiring the form-fitting skirt and matching blouse.

"Thank you. I wasn't sure about the color."

"No, light blue looks wonderful on you."

"You look dapper yourself."

Eric looked down at his dark blue three-button suit with thin orange pinstripes. "You don't think this orange tie looks gay, huh?"

"It's very *GQ*."

"Thanks."

Eric's hands caught her eye. She reached over and touched one. "Nice manicure. Mr. Swift, are you a metrosexual?"

"No." He winked his eye. "Just sexual."

"Oh my," Eden laughed, while fanning herself with a napkin.

"So, Ms. Eden Alexander. Tell me about yourself."

She put down her fork and took a sip of wine. "Hmm, what would you like to know, Mr. Swift?"

Eric smiled. *Oh, she wants to flirt,* he thought.

"I want to know everything. All the dirt. In fact, I even want to know about the mud." He grinned.

"No dirt here. I'm clean." She winked.

I bet. I can't wait to smell how clean, Eric thought. "Okay," he said. "Tell me something about yourself that only a few people would know."

"Why should I tell you?" She smacked her lips, teasing.

Eric adjusted his tie. " 'Cause I'm trustworthy."

"Really?" Eden said, unconvinced.

"I'm serious," he assured her. "For years, mothers and fathers all over the country have slept easy knowing that I was taking care of their daughters."

Yeah, but did the daughters sleep easy? Eden thought. "Okay, Mr. Trustworthy," she began, "here's something that very few people know about me."

He scooted his chair up and leaned into the table. "Ooh, this sounds like it's going to be good."

"I used to be a *Soul Train* dancer."

"What? Get the hell outta here."

"I'm serious," she deadpanned.

Back in the day, I wanted to sleep with that fly Chinese chick with the long hair that used to dance on Soul Train, Eric thought, before quickly refocusing on the woman he would like to get with now. "Damn, you got any tapes of you dancing?"

Eden frowned. "Uh, no."

"Well then," Eric said, grabbing his cell phone. "I got to call Don Cornelius." They both laughed.

It was Eden's turn to ask a question. "Now, Mr. Swift. Tell me something that only a few people know about you."

"I used to be a woman," Eric deadpanned.

Eden nearly spit out her wine. "Boy, shut up. You are crazy. Be serious."

"Alright. I have an addiction, a very serious addiction."

Eden put her fork down, her smile replaced with a look of concern. "Really? What is it?"

"Books," Eric admitted rather sheepishly.

"Huh?" she asked.

"I'm hooked on books. I read like two books a week sometimes."

Eden sighed in relief. She thought he was going to say he was hooked on drugs. "What kind of books?"

"All types but mainly history, science, and spiritual books."

I never would've guessed that. Maybe I'm wrong about Mr. Swift, she thought. "You're spiritual?" Eden said with a sly grin.

"It's something my father instilled in me. You seem surprised."

"I just wouldn't have guessed that. You always seem so—"

"Silly?" he interjected.

"Carefree is what I'm thinking."

Eric stopped smiling and looked deep into Eden's eyes. "I don't believe in letting the world in on my world."

Eden pursed her lips. "Why are you sharing this with me then?"

He placed his hand on top of hers. "You make me want to share my world."

She blushed. "You don't even know me."

"I don't have to know you to know you."

Feeling flustered, she gently pulled her hand back. "Let's change the subject. What did you do before you got into television?"

Okay, Eric. Remember it's a marathon, not a sprint. "I was in the league," he said.

"The league? What's that?" Eden asked, looking over the rim of her wineglass.

"The NFL. I played cornerback for the Washington Redskins." *What is 'The league'? She bugging. She has to know I played pro ball. She ain't slick. She doesn't want to sweat me.*

"Oh, I'm not really into sports," Eden said. "Where did you go to college?"

"University of Miami. And you?"

"Spelman."

Eric topped off Eden's wineglass, then his own, and said, "Eden, even though you went to that stuck-up college in Atlanta, I'd still like to take you out again."

"My," she teased. "You are straightforward."

"I'm a go-getter," he said, then paused. A devilish grin crossed his lips. "And when I first saw you I said to myself, I'ma go get her."

That was cute. Corny but cute, she thought, then said, "We can go out again, but under one condition."

"What's that?" he asked.

"I pick the place."

"No problem. Where we going?"

Eden smiled. "We're going to church."

Eric gave Eden a slow smile. *She can't be serious*, he thought. *She must be testing me, but that's okay. The devil ain't afraid of visiting the house of the Lord.*

Chapter Seven

The following morning Eric was in his office struggling to get his leg out of his pants when he heard an instant message alert beep on his computer. He furiously hopped out of his pants and threw them on the couch. After his show, Eric always changed out of his suit into more comfortable clothes.

The computer alert chirped again. He leaned over and pressed his space button on the keyboard. "Damn, he just got my email?" Eric squinted as he sat down and read the message. He'd emailed LeBaron earlier that morning about his date with Eden.

"She's taking the devil to church?" was LeBaron's surprised reply. He'd been busy going through the online editions of the newspapers in his office, and had just gotten a chance to read Eric's message. He laughed so hard when he opened it he nearly knocked over the mug of coffee on his desk. While he waited for Eric to respond, he sent a second message. "Well . . . what are you going to do?"

"I'm taking my black ass to church," Eric messaged back immediately.

"Why did I even ask?" LeBaron grinned. "You'd do whatever for the booty."

"That is tru," Eric misspelled. He was trying to type with one hand and eat a bacon, egg, and cheese sandwich. His after-show ritual consisted of the sandwich, a cup of hot chocolate, and answering emails or sending pornographic jokes to LeBaron. "However," Eric continued to peck away at the keyboard, "and don't fall out of yor chair, but I think it's a grat idea. I've been living extra foul lately and chuch might do me some god."

Eric's phone rang. He pressed the speakerphone button. "Hello?" he said.

"Nigga, have you lost your mind?" LeBaron cracked through the line.

"Hmm?" Eric mumbled, his mouth full.

"Lemme get this straight." LeBaron stood and closed his office door for privacy. "You are going to church and nobody died or is getting married?"

"Yep," Eric gulped, washing down a mouthful of hot chocolate. "I'm serious, LeBaron. I've really been evaluating my spirituality, and I have to be honest with you, I'm lacking."

Silence.

"LeBaron?"

"I'm here. I'm just stunned."

"What? You think that you and Phoenix are the only ones who can go to church?"

"No, bruh. But I've known you for damn near ten years and I've never once heard you question your own spirituality."

"C'mon, bruh. How you gon' say that? You know the type of stuff I read."

"Yeah, E, I know you're a freak for books but . . ." LeBaron paused. "Hey man, forget it. I'm happy to hear you talk like that."

"Thanks, bruh," Eric said, wiping his mouth with the back of his hand. "But if I go through all of this and don't get any sex out of the deal, I ain't going back to church until Easter."

"I guess you could say that I'ma go-getter," Eric said later that night, attempting to whisper into the curvaceous woman's ear. He was at happy hour at Club Traffik, Manhattan's new "it" club of the moment. Eric was there to hook up with Doug Bennett, a party promoter and one of his college buddies who kept him up on the hot new clubs.

The sexy woman backed her ass in closer, grinding her hips to Bounty Killer's new dance hall smash. She danced like she was auditioning for the dance hall king's next video.

"What did you say?" she yelled over her shoulder.

Damn, she smells good, he thought.

Eric put both his hands on her hips and pulled her even closer. "You said I'm aggressive. And I said I'ma go-getter. And when I saw you I said to myself that I was going to go and get her."

She laughed and looked down at his hands wrapped around her shapely hips. "Looks like you got me." She bent forward in a half doggy style, her ample ass grinding on his bulge.

"Oh shit. You dropping it like it's hot. You ready to get out of here?"

She turned around and hugged him. She had a huge smile on her face and her eyes were glassy. "I was ready when I first saw you."

It took Eric less than twenty minutes to hook up with Giselle. Happy hour at Club Traffik on Manhattan's East Side was a meat market of beautiful flesh. He had spotted her almost as soon as he walked in the door. Standing with three attractive Hispanic-looking girlfriends in VIP, Giselle, wearing a turquoise form-fitting skirt and top, stood out like a peacock in a group of chickens.

From across the room, Eric thought J-Lo was in the club. As he walked by and her features came into focus, he realized she wasn't J-Lo. But he was not disappointed.

While she went to the restroom Eric spotted his friend Doug by the bar. "Where you been? I've been looking for you," Eric said.

"I've been right here watching you get your mack on."

"You see the ass on her?"

"Word. Her name is Giselle."

"Gazelle? What kind of name is that?"

Doug laughed and waved the bartender over. "No, Giselle. She's Dominican or some shit like that."

"You hit that?" Eric asked, wondering how Doug knew her.

"Nigga, I wish. I've seen her at some of my parties. She's been in a few videos."

"I'll put her phat ass in a video."

"Word."

Posted up by the bar, the two men sipped their drinks and surveyed the room. The club's manager came over to talk to Doug. While they talked, Eric approached Giselle and asked her to dance again.

Five Captain Morgans and Cokes later they were in a cab headed to her place uptown. Eric never brought one-night stands to his place. And this was definitely looking like a one-nighter.

Giselle lived in Harlem on 121st Street and Manhattan Avenue, just a few blocks from the famous Apollo Theater. As the driver turned off 125th Street, Eric looked out the cab window with a shocked expression on his face. Where run-down storefronts used to be now stood a Starbucks, HMV store, and a Magic Johnson Movie Theater.

"This shit look like Times Square," Eric said.

"Never been to Harlem?" Giselle asked.

"Of course, I'm from the Bronx. But I haven't been

back here in a few years. Shit, ain't look like this back in the day."

"Yeah, white people buying up everything in Harlem," she said. "Yo, I have like four white people living on my block."

Her block was nice. Two rows of refurbished brownstones faced each other on a street that had very few parked cars on it. Giselle unlocked the door to her place, and they walked inside her apartment. The air, or what there was of it, was thick and stuffy. Her dirty apartment was large, with clothes or junk covering nearly every square foot. The place looked like it was decorated by *Better Homes and Garbage*.

"Excuse the mess. I didn't plan on company."

"Girl . . . I don't care about your apartment." He slurred his words seductively while pinching her ass. "Do you have a bed?"

"Yeah."

"What size?"

"King-size."

Eric squeezed his crotch. "Just the right size for this king cobra." They both laughed.

"Want a beer? All I got is Corona," she asked.

"Corona is all I need."

Eric watched as Giselle opened the refrigerator. He couldn't keep his eyes off her. He saw her grab a bottle of water and wash down a pill. "You got a headache?" he asked.

She laughed and did a very wobbly pirouette. "No, silly, I feel great."

Great, 'cause I definitely want some ass. Eric got up, walked into the kitchen, and grabbed a small pink pill out of Giselle's hand.

"Girl, what are you taking?"

"X."

"X? As in Ecstasy?"

"Yeah. You want one?" she asked, wrapping her arms around him.

"Hell, nah. I don't want any of that. That shit'll kill you."

"No it won't. It's the best. I do it all the time."

"Whatever. That shit be having niggas directing traffic on the Brooklyn Bridge in their drawers."

Giselle laughed for a long time. Too damn long. Eric looked at his watch. It was only 11 PM. He could still go back to the club. *This bitch is a crackhead. I'm outta here*, he thought, heading for the door.

"You don't know what you're missing. This shit is the bomb. And sex on E is hot. Ay, Papi?"

Eric froze. "What about sex on E?" he said.

"On X, I can suck dick for hours."

He turned around. "Suck dick for hours?"

She licked her lips. "Hours."

"What will it do for me?"

She smiled. "You'll be able to fuck me for hours."

"Girl, gimme one of them things."

47

Forty-five minutes later, Eric yawned and a wave of euphoria rushed though his entire body. It felt like one giant never-ending orgasm. He was sitting in a chair and had on nothing but his shoes and shirt. Giselle was sucking his dick like he was her man.

"Who are you?" he said, his mind foggy from the X.

Giselle took his dick out of her mouth. "Giselle, silly." She laughed.

GGGisselllle . . . siillllyyy, the name echoed in his mind. He stared at the top of her head. It was bouncing like a bobble-head doll.

"Who is she?" Eric said, pointing to the left. Giselle ignored him. He was seeing double. *Damn, this X shit is the bomb*, he thought.

Time flew by. Eric looked at his watch. It was 4 AM. After five hours of porno-style sex, Giselle was passed out. Eric lay beside her in the bed. He was wide awake and couldn't remember anything. He rubbed his knees. He wondered why they burned. He smacked his lips. *Uck! Taste like somebody took a shit in my mouth. Oh my God, I hope she didn't piss on me.*

Eric glanced at her and lightly slapped her ass. Her body was still, except for the one cheek jiggling. He hoped she wasn't dead.

Eight times. I came eight times. And I'm still hard. I can't believe it.

Eric stared at the water-stained tiles hanging from the ceiling. In his groggy and high state it looked as if the roof was about to collapse. He closed his eyes and tried to sleep. He was imagining things that he couldn't describe. Suddenly, he felt a quick thump on his chest.

He jerked upright, throwing the sheet off him. "What the hell?" he said. He looked around the room. Nothing. He looked at Giselle. She was snoring. "How can she sleep high on X and I'm bugging out?" he muttered to the room.

Eric pulled the sheets up to his neck. His nervous gaze darted around the room. Fifteen minutes later, again he felt a thump, thump, thump across his chest. Eric jumped up again. This time he furiously brushed off his chest. Naked, covering his privates with his hand, he got out of bed. Grabbing an umbrella from a corner, he knelt and cautiously looked under the bed. There was nothing under it except enough junk to make Sanford and Son jealous. Gripping the umbrella like a baseball bat, he tiptoed into the living room and flicked on the light. He scanned the room. He scanned the large apartment. Clothes were strewn all over the plastic-covered couch and floor.

I ain't fucking with X no more. This shit got me tripping. Where are my drawers?

He found them by the couch along with his pants. He turned to walk back to the bedroom and stepped right into a bucket of Kentucky Fried Chicken. It was greasy and filled with gnawed chicken bones, stripped to the gristle. Eric kicked the bucket, muttering, "What is a bucket of chicken doing on the floor?"

He walked over to the front door and flicked that switch. Light flooded the adjacent kitchen. The sink was filled with crusty dishes.

"This is some raggedy-ass shit. I'm getting the fuck outta here." He looked at his watch. 4:37 AM. "Shit. Ain't no cabs up in Harlem at this time of morning."

Eric went back to bed. This time he pulled the sheets over his head. Just as he was starting to doze, he felt something wet on his big toe. His body froze. His eyes bulged until they were as wide and white as lightbulbs. Head still covered by the sheet, he looked like the bug-eyed shiftless Negro caricature, Stepin Fetchit.

I hope Giselle is sucking my toes, 'cause if she ain't, I'ma lose my goddamn mind.

Slowly Eric peeked from under the covers.

"Ah! A rat!" he screamed, jumping out of the bed. The rat ran toward him. He jumped back in the bed. "A goddamn rat? What the fuck!"

The rat ran into the living room. Standing in the bed, he nudged Giselle in the ribs with his foot. "Wake up! Wake the fuck up!"

Giselle was comatose. He jumped out of the bed again and started gathering his clothes. "I'm getting the fuck outta here. I don't give a fuck if I have to walk home."

As he closed the door he stole one final glance at the nasty apartment. All he could still hear was Giselle snoring.

Chapter Eight

Madison Square Garden, located on Thirty-fourth and Eighth Avenue, had for decades been famous for fight fans. Some of the most memorable matches in boxing history took place there. But on this Sunday morning, men weren't fighting each other. It was God versus the devil.

The match was taking place at the Sunday service of the fifth annual black Baptist convention. It was the last day of a weeklong conference featuring some of the biggest names in the black Baptist Church. Nearly a dozen of the most prominent preachers in the country were scheduled to speak. The crowds of black people seated in the Garden were dressed to impress. Nearly all the men wore suits. The outfits ranged from conservative black three-button suits to bright pimp red six-button ones, complete with matching alligator shoes. The women, never to be outdone, were decked out in everything from

Easter Sunday–worthy two-piece pastels with matching hats to skimpy black form-fitting skirts—their Sunday morning best that could have just as easily been worn on Saturday night.

"Damn, is that Bishop Magic Don Juan?" Eric nudged Eden and nodded in the direction of a man sitting a few rows down in front of them. The man had on a double-breasted money-green-colored suit with thick gold pin-stripes. A gold-tipped cane rested on his lap, twinkling just as brightly as the gold front tooth in his mouth.

Eden shrugged her shoulders and turned her gaze back to the stage. "I don't know who Bishop Juan is, but this is a Baptist convention and I don't think that a priest would be here."

Eric burst out laughing.

An elderly woman turned and shushed him. Eric stared back and was just about to say "Shut your old ass up" when Eden elbowed him.

"Pay attention. This choir is amazing."

This is some bullshit, he thought. *Why did I agree to this? My head is killing me. I have to quit drinking. I still feel high. That X is some wild shit.*

"I'm hungry," he said, rubbing his stomach. "You want to get something to eat after the service?"

Eden nodded her head yes.

Although Eric had been exposed to church at a young age, he had never attended on a regular basis. His mother went all the time, but his father was the family's resident religionist and Eric was his prized pupil. They liked CME services best—Christmas, Mother's Day, and Easter. At first Eric thought Eden was joking when she said their date would be at church. She really wanted him to hear her pastor, a hot young preacher who was scheduled to speak the last day of the convention. But it didn't matter to him in the least where they went or what they did. He'd once rode a bike sixteen miles across town and climbed rickety ladders for sex. This was a piece of cake. He scanned the crowd and the ministers on the stage. The whole scene reminded him of the circus.

Pops was right. Half these people are dressed like clowns and the preachers act like ringmasters.

The service opened with spotlights, a laser light show, and a choir with at least three hundred members. The emphasis seemed not to be on the Word, but on the Spectacle. In the last ten to fifteen years, celebrity ministers, megachurches, and Bible conferences in controversial places like Las Vegas and the Bahamas had become an issue within the black church community. Eric thought it felt like there was a big elephant in the room that nobody wanted to acknowledge.

Some fine-ass women in here, though. I might have to come to church more often. He laughed at himself, realizing it would be like Satan sitting in Sunday school. He eyed a thick sister with an hourglass shape clapping her hands and bouncing along with the choir. *She lucky I ain't got no singles.*

Scanning the crowd further, he saw groups of attractive

women sitting by themselves. Every time the middle-aged and very fat minister who was leading the choir exaggerated a verse, they screamed.

I'll make ya ass scream. I couldn't be a preacher. I'd be banging everything in here.

"What are you thinking about?" Eden asked.

"You don't want to know," he assured her.

Intrigued, she turned and faced him. "Oh, I do want to know."

"I'm wondering why way more women come to church than men."

Eden frowned. "You tell me."

"I don't know."

"Well, you should. You don't come to church. Why is that?"

Eric thought for a moment. "I guess I'm lazy."

Eden shook her head, then turned her attention back to the stage.

"There he is. That's my pastor," Eden said proudly.

"Where?" Eric asked, looking around.

"Down there." She pointed toward the stage. "He's about to speak. You are going to love him."

"How do you figure that?" Eric was skeptical.

"Just watch," she said confidently.

The Reverend Joshua Enoch Francois was about to give the biggest sermon of his short career. As he walked to the pulpit, scanning the nearly twenty thousand people filling the seats of Madison Square Garden, he prayed silently. *I will bless the Lord at all times; his praise shall continually be in my mouth.*

The gravity of the moment weighed heavily on the thirty-year-old junior minister from Harlem. He only had fifteen minutes to speak, so he had to go all out. Still, it was nearly unheard of for such a young man to address the conference. Joshua was a rising star in the Association of Black Baptist Ministers. His church, New Sunlight Baptist, and his youth ministry impressed many of the association's leaders. At a time when young people in New York City were turning away from the church in record numbers, he was converting them in droves.

Some of the more conservative and traditional preachers took issue with his controversial style. "Loose cannon" was a phrase often used to describe Joshua. But most knew that if the church was to stay relevant, they needed young people. Joshua spoke their language. It also helped that he was a former platinum rap star. To his fans he was Danger, a smooth hip-hop star who glorified the bling lifestyle. For a while his glitzy videos were in constant rotation on BET and MTV. His antics backstage and on tour were legendary. His last album, *Sex, Drugs and Hip-Hop*, was condemned by the very organization he was speaking before today.

His transformation happened one night after a show in Miami. The night ended with the usual debauchery. As he lay awake, too high from all the cocaine he'd ingested to sleep, he saw his surroundings in a new light. In his bed slept two naked women he'd never seen before and would never see again. Around the room were bags of weed and empty liquor bottles. A video camera was on, keeping record of the entire sordid night. But it was what was in the chair that had Danger transfixed. It was him. But how could he be in the bed and sitting in the chair at the same time? The figure in the chair was dressed in a fine golden robe, but he looked old, haggard, and lonely. Danger jumped out of bed and crept toward himself. The horrors he saw in his own eyes shook him to his soul.

He never revealed what he saw to anyone, but that night, he retired from rap. The press thought it was a publicity stunt, but Francois spent the next four years in a seminary studying the world's religions along with science, astronomy, and mathematics. Now he was back onstage.

The Garden was eerily quiet as he stood at the mahogany pulpit. *My soul shall make her boast in the Lord. The humble shall hear thereof and be glad.*

His right hand trembled slightly as he adjusted the microphone stand. The faint screech of feedback echoed throughout the room. His heartbeat thumped loudly in his ears. He carefully placed his notes on the podium. Every eye was on him. Eyes that were sizing him up. Eyes that were waiting for him to fail. Joshua looked more like a banker than a preacher. He wore a navy blue three-button suit. His light blue shirt was a perfect canvas for the red, navy, and light blue striped tie. Everything blended. Joshua always had a talent for blending in. He was neither handsome nor unattractive. His hairstyle, a low cut, even-all-over fade, was neither flashy nor simple. But he was blessed with a great skin tone, thanks to his Louisiana Creole mixed with Caribbean ancestry. The girls used to call him Chocolate. But that was a long time ago.

Joshua sipped from a glass of water and cleared his throat.

O magnify the Lord with me and let us exalt his name together. I sought the Lord and he heard me and delivered me from all my fears.

He bowed his head. "Pray with me."

Everyone bowed their heads.

"Lord, I pray for the wisdom of Solomon and that mankind is blessed with the same. I pray for the patience of Job. I pray that I may live up to my responsibilities like a good man. I pray for the discipline, perseverance, and love of your son, Jesus Christ. Finally, I pray for the strength and courage of all the just kings, queens, and warriors of history. Amen."

"Amen," said the crowd.

"I bet you've never heard that prayer before," Joshua said.

The crowd smiled. Somewhere a voice yelled out, "Don't matter, it's all G-O-D."

"Then I guess it was all good," Joshua shot back.

The crowd laughed.

He continued. "I'll tell you why you've never heard that prayer before. It's because I made it up. Yeah, I make up prayers. I don't care."

He closed the open Bible he held in his palms. "There are other prayers not in this great and holy book."

A few of the ministers on the stage shot concerned glances at each other. Uh-oh, the cannon was loose.

"Ain't nothing wrong with making up your own prayers. Ya'll do it all the time. But you can't be making up no prayers like, 'Lord, bless me with a candy apple–red BMW sitting on chrome twenty-twos.' "

Waves of laughter rolled through the Garden. A few people sat up straighter in their seats.

"Or better yet, 'Lord bless me with a man who has a candy apple red BMW sitting on chrome twenty-twos.' "

More laughter.

"Oh, some pastors say, 'Joshua, boy, you better stick to the Gospels. Stick to the Word.' You know what I tell them?"

"To leave you alone?" someone in the crowd yelled.

He ignored the man and said, "I tell them the Word is right here." Joshua pointed to his heart. "I'ma tell you something that is going to make a lot of preachers mad."

He smiled at the row of older pastors sitting behind him. Some smiled back nervously. Some stared.

"You don't need any of us to talk to God," he said with a dramatic sweep of his hand.

"That's right," an older woman sitting in the front row yelled. "You don't need nobody but Jesus."

A few of the elderly preachers nervously scratched the backs of their heads.

Way in the back, a man stood, pointed his finger, and said, "Preach, young man, preach."

Joshua cleared his throat. "That's right, I said it. How do they say it in St. Louis? I don't curr!"

Even the preachers laughed at the young man's attempt at Midwest Ebonics.

"You don't need a middleman to talk to God. Moses didn't need one. Jesus didn't need one. God is inside all of us. God wants to talk to you. Don't matter who you are. God doesn't have caller ID. Those whispers you hear in your head when you're alone? That's God talking to you."

Joshua paused.

"Hold on, lemme clarify. That whisper that you hear when you're alone that's telling you to do right? That's God. Now, all of that nasty stuff you're also hearing in your head? That's the devil."

The crowd broke up again with laughter.

"A lot of ya'll know what I'm talking about." Joshua waved his finger at the crowd. "Some of ya'll hearing the voice now. I guarantee you a lot of men didn't come here to see me. They wanted to see these fine pretty women."

Eric nearly bit his lip to keep from smiling.

"They be saying, 'Oh my God, look at her ass . . . sets, and they probably came here to church with a woman. I'm here to tell you, brother, that's foul. That voice in your head? 'Man, they got some fine women in church. Let's go check them out.' That's the devil, brother. And I know the devil quite well. The devil used to talk to me all the time. The devil still talks to me. These days I just don't listen."

The crowd roared. Joshua unhooked the cordless microphone from the stand. He walked from behind the podium. Joshua's image seemed larger than life on the Garden's giant screen.

"Oh, but I used to listen."

Hoots and yells filled the Garden.

Joshua's voice rose. It sounded powerful and old. "I'ma tell you another thing a lot of preachers ain't gon' like."

"What's that, preacher?" A heavyset black woman wearing an eye patch and a big yellow Easter hat bellowed. Eric thought she looked like a big fat pretty pastel pirate.

Again, Joshua smiled and looked at the row of preachers. Then he turned and faced the crowd.

"I've smoked more weed than Cheech and Chong."

The crowd laughed like they were at a Chris Rock show.

"Oh, my Lord," one of the older pastors whispered to an even older pastor sitting next to him.

Joshua continued. "That's right. And I've snorted more cocaine than Scarface."

Some of the preachers shook their heads.

"Drank more gin and juice than Snoop Dogg. Matter of fact, I drank gin and juice *with* Snoop Dogg."

"That boy is crazy," Joshua heard one of the preachers whisper.

"Ya'll know how I was. You read it in the papers. Seen it

on TV. I was a buck-wild rap star. My nickname was Danger. That ain't all. I've also hollered at more women than Bishop Magic Don Juan."

Eric was beside himself laughing.

"You know what my favorite color use to be for a woman?"

He paused while the crowd quieted down.

"Ya'll ain't hearing me. I said, know what my favorite color use to be for a woman?"

"What color?" the crowd yelled.

"Buck naked," Joshua said, curling his lips into an ugly half frown–half grin. It was pandemonium in the Garden.

Eric elbowed Eden. "I love this nigga."

"Watch your mouth, Eric," she replied.

Joshua walked to the edge of the stage. His face was serious. "I didn't start going to church until I was twenty-six years old. Oh, I went to weddings and a few funerals, but regular church service? Oh no. You had to trick me to get me in church. Like tell me they having happy hour or something. I'm not telling you this to make you laugh. I want you to know that you too can talk to God. I did. My life had sunk so low it couldn't go any lower. When I heard the voice of God, I answered it. I didn't have to go to no preacher first. I went straight to God. I heard his voice in my mind; it was a powerful voice. It had to be for me to hear it through all that weed, all that coke, all that gin and juice. It had to be powerful to drown out the voice of that pretty woman I was shacking up with.

"After I got right with God, then I went to the preacher. The preacher is here to instruct you on the interpretation of the Word, but the preacher ain't the Word. God is the Word." He checked his chronowatch—fourteen minutes. He walked back to his seat and smiled at a row of very mad preachers.

When Eric and Eden exited the Garden an hour later, Eric couldn't shut up about Reverend Francois's sermon. After a while Eden had zoned him out. He was still talking twenty minutes later when they exited the cab in front of a restaurant. He and Eden were having dinner at the Red Eye Grill in midtown Manhattan. As they waited for their table, Eric continued to talk nonstop. Eden turned and shook her head in amazement.

"My, you've just been Mr. Chatty tonight," Eden teased. "I couldn't get in a word during the cab ride."

"I can't help it. Reverend Francois has me geeked."

"Oh really? I wouldn't have noticed."

"I might go to church if he was my pastor."

Eden looked him in the eye. "What's stopping you from going to his church?"

His eyes nervously glanced around the restaurant. "Um, look, our table is ready. I'm hungrier than an Ethiopian on the Atkins diet," Eric said to the waiter as he slid into the booth.

Eden, her face partially covered by the menu, grinned.

Eric ordered a rib eye well done and a Captain Morgan and Coke. Eden ordered the chicken Caesar salad and a glass of white wine, and the waiter took their menus.

"I'm glad you enjoyed yourself at the service," she said.

"Sorry, but that preacher was crazy. I've never heard anyone preach like that. It was a refreshing change from the normal buck-jumping chicken George style preaching."

Eden opened her compact and checked her lipstick, then said, "All churches aren't like that."

He shrugged his shoulders. "Black churches are."

She snapped her compact shut. "No, they're not."

"And most of the preachers are crooks."

"Goodness gracious," Eden said. "Why are people always so caught up in what the pastor is doing? You heard Reverend Francois. Go to God first."

"Whatever." Eric smirked. "Most of them preachers who were up there gon' go to hell."

"I'm surprised at you, Eric," she said, unfolding a napkin. "How do you figure that?"

Eric was nonplussed as he sipped his water. "Look, any preacher who wears a canary yellow and black plaid suit is doing something that's gon' land his ass in hell."

Eden sighed. "Again, why are we as black people always concerned about how the preacher looks or what he's doing? It's the message, not the man."

"Oh God," Eric said, rolling his eyes. "That's a cop-out. How can you not worry about what the preacher is doing? Hell, he got his hands out asking me for money, and his suit cost more than mine. Five damn offerings? I went to my cousin's wedding at this church in Atlanta. The preacher asked for an offering at the wedding."

Eden giggled. "No, he didn't. I'm from Atlanta. What's the name of the church?"

"I don't know. It was a big-ass church. Twenty thousand members. It had a damn ATM in the lobby!"

Eden covered her mouth with her hand to keep from howling. People nearby glanced at them.

"Boy, stop it! You're gonna make me scream."

He ignored her plea. "An ATM right next to a Taco Bell. Why is there a Taco Bell in a church lobby? Are they drinking Pepsi and substituting chalupas for communion crackers? I'm telling you, these black churches ain't nothing but a scam."

Eden shook her head in mock disgust. "My, Mr. Swift, I didn't know that you were so cynical."

"I'm not cynical, just realistic. I used to go to this church every now and then when I was in college. The preacher was a young cat who used to wear thousand-dollar suits. Nigga had a Duke kit in his hair. This is ninety-four or -five. Who in the hell was still wearing a Duke kit in the mid-nineties?"

Eden was trying hard not to lose it.

"So anyway, for his fifth anniversary the deacons and the church chipped in and bought him a Five Series black BMW convertible with chrome rims and leather interior.

Tell me, why in the hell does a preacher need a convertible Beemer?"

It was Eden's turn to shrug her shoulders.

"Always talking about being Christlike. Jesus ain't ride in a BMW. He rode a damn donkey."

Eden burst out laughing.

"Oh, and guess what? He got caught cheating on his wife in his office at church."

Eden's eyes bugged. "In church?"

Eric arched his right eyebrow for emphasis. "Yes. I guess he was saving hos' souls."

Later that afternoon, Eric dropped Eden off at her apartment. After opening the passenger-side door, he left his Mercedes S500 double-parked and walked her up the steps to her apartment door.

"This is one of the best dates I have ever had," he said, looking into her eyes.

She arched her eyebrow. "This wasn't a date."

"No." He frowned. "Well, what would you call it?"

Eden was silent as she unlocked her door.

"Well?" Eric pressed her.

She smiled. "Let's call it a probationary hearing."

Eric was speechless as the door slammed in his face. Eden turned and winked at him through the glass.

Probation, huh, he thought. *I don't want no damn probation. I want life with her without a chance for parole.*

Chapter Nine

The next morning, Eden was bored as she watched her coanchor, Ryan Sanchez, interview the New Jersey attorney general.

She was also pissed.

He's interviewing the attorney general? I should be doing that interview. But instead I get the weird lady from the animal shelter. Eden sighed and checked the studio clock. *It's six fifty-four? Feels like I've been on the air all day. I hate Monday mornings.*

Unbeknownst to Eden, inside the control room chaos was brewing.

"Ryan. I need you to stretch," a producer said in Ryan's earpiece. The anchor nodded imperceptibly.

Why do they want him to stretch? Eden thought.

She was about to find out.

"Eden? Listen up, we have breaking news," a deep male voice calmly said through her earpiece.

She immediately perked up. "Bryan, is that you?" she lip-synched to the control room monitor so the producers could see her.

"Yes. Pay attention," Bryan ordered. "Write this down." Bryan Cole was the executive producer of the morning show. For him to be in the control room, the breaking news must be big.

His instructions were short and clear, a throwback to his army days. "Ten minutes ago. Shots fired inside City Hall. Lone gunman. A number of people may have been hit, including a city councilman."

Eden, her blood pressure rising, furiously scribbled.

While she caught up, Bryan asked the director if they had Chopper 7's signal. They did.

"Eden," he continued. "Gunman is still inside City Hall. Don't know if he's caught. Chopper is there. You will talk over pictures. You're doing it next. Got it?"

Eden nodded. *Hurry up and say good-bye, Ryan.*

"New Jersey State Attorney General John Hollins," Ryan said. "Thank you for joining us. Eden, back to you."

"We have breaking news to report. Chopper Seven is over the scene. It's chaos inside and outside City Hall after gunfire erupts. We are told a number of people may have been shot, including a city councilman."

"And a police officer," Bryan whispered in her ear.

"And a police officer," Eden said, not missing a beat.

"Sources tell channel seven that about ten to fifteen minutes ago, a lone gunman managed to somehow get a gun through metal detectors and the mandatory pat down and start shooting. At this time we have no motive for the shooting."

"We're staying with this," Bryan said in her ear.

"Folks, we are going to stay with this picture as this scene develops."

"Cops are blocking the streets," Bryan told her.

"Folks, this is a serious situation, and if you have any business near the courthouse, you should definitely stay away until police get a handle on this. As you can see from these pictures, police officers are blocking the streets."

"That's my girl," Bryan said.

Ryan, by this time, had made it back to the desk and was anxious to get in on the coverage. He waved at the control room monitor that he was going to jump in. He touched Eden's arm.

Eden paused. *What is he doing?*

"Folks, this is Ryan Sanchez. As you may remember, I recently did a two-part series on the disrepair and lack of metal detectors in many of the city's buildings. Now I'm not saying that this is the case today, but that certainly is a valid question to be asked in light of what just happened."

Damn, Eden thought, *I need some new information. He is not going to run this coverage.*

Just then Bryan gave her some. As Ryan paused to catch his breath, Eden jumped right in.

"Excuse me, Ryan, but I'm getting some new information from my producers in the control room. We have confirmation that a city councilman is in fact dead. Folks, we know his name but will withhold that information until the next of kin has been notified."

From the corner of her eye, Eden saw Ryan shoot a very pissed look at the control room monitor.

"Uh-oh, somebody's pissed," Bryan said out loud. Everyone in the control room laughed.

Bryan looked at the clock. 6:58:07. The network's morning show would automatically come on at 7:00:00.

"Stay with this," Bryan told both anchors. They had less than two minutes left. Eden immediately began repeating the breaking news for viewers who were just tuning in to the show.

Bryan picked up the phone and called Karen Hunter, his news director, to find out if he could extend the show past seven o'clock. She was on a different line with the station's general manager, who was in a conference call with the president of network news. They were all watching the coverage.

6:59. Shit. Come on, Bryan thought. Everyone in the control room was looking at him, waiting on a decision.

After nearly a minute of high-level horse-trading, Karen came back on the line. "The network wants the story. Stay on until seven fifteen. Not a second later," she said.

Bryan hung up the phone. He looked at the clock.

6:59:50. He pressed the red ALL button. "Everybody listen up. We're staying on until seven fifteen."

"Over network?" the director asked.

"Did I stutter?" Bryan said, clearly annoyed.

"Are you ready for your fifteen minutes of fame?" he whispered in Eden's earpiece.

She had a Mount Rushmore–like stare on her face.

A national audience. Thank you, God, Eden thought as she tossed to a reporter on the phone who was live from the scene.

The station had cut into programming periodically throughout the morning with reports anchored by Eden. All totaled, she had been on the air live for nearly two hours and still didn't want to leave the anchor desk. The normal noon anchor team had to pry her off the set. Eden was exhilarated by the whole experience. It finally gave her a chance to flex her skills.

Eric, excited and proud of Eden, asked her out for coffee.

"You were awesome out there this morning," he said, sipping on a double latte. "I was really impressed."

"Really?" Eden asked. "I felt like I could have done better."

Eric slurped the last of the flavored coffee. "C'mon. You were masterful. Did you see Ryan's face? I think he was jealous."

A mischievous smile crossed her face. "You think?"

Eric nodded. "If there is one thing that I know, it's egos."

She didn't have time to worry about bruised egos. "I just hope the network brass saw it."

The two were at a nearby Barnes and Noble bookstore, located in nearby Lincoln Square. The megabookstore was one of Eric's favorite haunts. He couldn't walk by the store without dipping in and buying a book or three.

Eden admired the stack of books Eric had just purchased. "You sure read a lot."

"All the time," he said proudly.

"You must spend a lot of time here."

"Every Sunday morning this is where you can find me."

Eden smiled. "Me at church and you at the bookstore."

Eric rubbed his chin and thought about what she had said. "Well, we have a lot in common then."

"What?"

"Both of us are seeking knowledge."

Eden stirred her iced coffee. "You know something, Eric. You are not what I expected."

He straightened up, intrigued by her comment. "Oh, and what did you expect?"

"Well, you know how most successful ex–ball players are."

He was silent.

"But you're . . . you're such a contradiction. Always joking at work, flirting with me . . . you wear such nice and expensive clothes." She paused, smiling. "And I know you like to party, but here you are with books about subjects that I can't even understand."

"Well, you know what they say."

"No, what do they say?"

"Never judge a book by its cover."

"Eric, do you have a girlfriend?"

"Umm . . ." He coughed, momentarily taken aback by the question. After gathering his thoughts, he smiled and said, "No, at least not yet. What about you?" he asked. "Do you have a man?"

"I haven't really had the time."

"I don't really need much time," he said, looking at his watch.

Eden smiled. "What are your thoughts about marriage and kids?"

"Honestly, I haven't really thought about them at all."

"You should. You're not getting any younger," Eden teased.

"You sound like my best friend, LeBaron."

"What does he say?"

"That I should settle down."

"He sounds like a smart guy."

"Yeah." Eric stared at his coffee. "Marriage has made LeBaron a real smart guy."

"You don't sound convinced."

Eric smiled. "I don't know, marriage works for some people."

Eden eyed him hard. "What about you?"

He suddenly glanced at his watch. "Whew, look at the time. We better get back to work."

As they got up to leave, Eden grabbed Eric's arm. "I'll let you off the hook this time, but next time you won't be so lucky."

Eric smiled nervously, all the while thinking, *Next time I'll have a better lie prepared.*

Chapter Ten

That night Eric was tucking his shirt in his pants when his cell phone rang. It was the third time in the last ten minutes. He ignored it and continued to groove to "Knee Deep," an old-school funk jam by Parliament Funkadelic. On beat, he splashed on a dash of BLV, one of his favorite brands of cologne, made by Bulgari. He had to smell extra nice tonight. He and his friend Dirty Dre had a double date. With some strippers.

"Boy, I hope Dirty is ready for some jelly," he joked at his reflection. Eric was taking Dre to The Goat, one of his favorite and craziest gentlemen's clubs.

The cell phone rang again.

"Damn, who is this?" He frowned while inspecting the caller ID. He turned down the music.

"Oh, snap. LeBaron, what's up?"

"We might lose the baby."

"Huh? Slow down, man, what are you talking about?"

"Phoenix is having problems and we might lose the baby."

Eric pulled the lid down on the toilet and sat down. "What's wrong?"

"She has something that's called preeclampsia."

"Pre what?" Eric said.

"It's called preeclampsia. It's a disease that can affect the organs."

"Damn, what causes it?" Eric asked.

"The doctors don't really know."

Eric was silent. For once he was at a loss for words.

"I'm scared, Eric."

"Hey man, don't be scared. You're the churchgoing man, remember? God loves you too much to hurt you. Phoenix hasn't lost the baby yet, right?"

"Nah," LeBaron said absently.

"Well then, let's take it one day at a time. We gon' pray about it and stay positive. Remember, you got family here, so keep me updated. You need me to come down?"

"Nah, man, but thanks for the offer and the prayers. By the way, I hear 'Knee Deep' playing in the background. Where you going?"

"As they say in the Dirty South, I'm fittin' to go the Scrip club."

"I'm telling you, Dirty, you should have gotten drunk," Eric said, pulling into the nightclub's parking lot. "Or smoked some of this bomb-ass weed." He took one last long drag on the blunt rolled up in a chocolate-flavored Phillie's Blunt cigar wrapper before putting it out in the ashtray.

Dirty Dre frowned. It was the fourth time Eric had made the remark about Dre getting drunk.

"N-n-n-nigga, this ain't my first time going to a strip club."

Eric laughed and couldn't resist teasing his boy. "That may be true, but you ain't never been to a strip club like The G-G-G-Goat. I promise you that."

"F-f-fuck you," Dirty stuttered. He stashed the nearly empty bottle of Rémy Martin under the front seat. "I can handle The Goat. Let's see if them bitches in The Goat can handle D-D-Dirty Dre."

The Goat was one of the hottest gentlemen's clubs in the city. It was also one of the most exclusive and expensive. You had to be a member or come with one. The price of fun was steep. For one thousand dollars, a man could party at The Goat all night and have damn near everything done to him.

Eric knocked on the door three times and a slit at eye level opened. A pair of red eyes stared out. Eric whispered something cryptic.

"What kind of James B-B-Bond shit is this?" Dirty Dre muttered.

After a thorough frisking by a very large bouncer, the two men walked into the main bar area.

"Oh my G-G-G," Dirty Dre gasped.

"It's okay, Dirty." Eric patted his friend on the back. "Just calm down."

There were at least one hundred women milling about the large area. Some were waitressing, some were bartending, some were dancing. All of them were buck naked.

His eyes big as paper plates, Dirty grabbed Eric's arm. "These b-b-bitches ain't got no clothes on."

"Um, that's the idea, Dirty," Eric said.

Dirty Dre stared around the club like a wide-eyed tourist. His heart was pounding, and he was as nervous as a thirteen-year-old virgin.

"I need a d-d-drink," he said, heading for the bar.

"I told you." Eric laughed.

After drinking two Heinekens and one Long Island iced tea, Dirty was ready for action. The alcohol also eased his stutter.

"Come with me. I want to show you something," Eric told him.

They walked down a dark hallway. The atmosphere was surreal. Hip-hop music thumped through dozens of speakers. Multicolored lights bounced off what the patrons called the Wall of Fame, rows of glass cases built into the walls with beautiful naked women dancing behind them. They were rubbing their hands all over their fantastic bodies and licking their lips.

"What do they do?" Dirty said, rubbing his hands together. His grin was devilish.

"Anything you want."

"Yeah? I could just pick one?" He blew a kiss at one of the girls. She stuck about a foot of tongue out back at him. Dirty Dre gulped.

"Or two," Eric added. "However many you can handle."

Dirty Dre shook his head in disbelief. "Where do you take them?"

"Follow me."

Eric took him into a large empty room that had three hallways. A tall gorgeous Dominican woman was standing in the middle of the room wearing a red see-through mesh bra and thong set. Her erect pierced nipples poked through the mesh. She made a sweeping motion with her arm.

"Which way do you want to go? The choice is yours," she said in accented English.

Dirty Dre looked at Eric for help.

"It don't matter," Eric said.

"Let's g-g-go that way," Dirty Dre said. The stutter had returned.

The woman smiled. "Ah, the Hall of Surprises," she said.

"I like s-s-surprises," Dirty said.

They walked down the hall, which reminded the two men of a hotel—in hell. The halls were smoky and bathed in an eerie red light. Every twelve to fifteen feet was an open door. Women of various shades, nationalities, and levels of undress stood in each doorway. Dirty Dre nearly jumped into the first room.

"Hold on, Dirty," Eric said, grabbing his arm. "Damn, don't jump at the first thing."

Dirty Dre shrugged and waved good-bye to the naked beauty sitting on the edge of a bed filing her fingernails. A second later Dirty ran back, stuck his head in, and whispered, "I'll be b-b-back."

They walked by the first three doors, then paused at the fourth. No one was at the door. They peeked inside. "Oh my God," both of them gasped.

Inside the room was a hot tub overflowing with bubbles. Splashing in it were near perfect doubles of Halle Berry and Pamela Anderson. They were topless and their perfect C and double D cups bounced like soapy softballs.

"Hey, guys," the girls said.

"Hey, girls," the guys said.

"You guys want to party?" Pamela said, holding up a chilled bottle of Cristal champagne.

The boys nodded.

"Come in."

They got stuck in the door trying to come in at the same time. Eric started to pull his shirt off. Dirty Dre bent down to untie his shoes.

Halle and Pamela stood up to make room for them.

Eric froze. "What the f-f-fuck?" he stuttered. He rubbed his eyes, trying to focus.

Dirty ignored him. He was too busy pulling his pants down.

"Oh w-w-wee," Dirty sang, looking down at his dick. "One of these bitches is gonna j-j-jerk it with Jergens."

Eric grabbed his shirt and ran out of the room, knocking Dirty down on his way out.

Dirty sat on the floor, confused. "Hey, where . . . ?"

He turned back to Halle and Pamela. "What the fuck?" Dre screamed, before grabbing his pants and shoes and dashing out into the hallway in his underwear.

Halle and Pamela stood in the tub frowning. Soapsuds dripped down their breasts and both of their enormous dicks.

Eric and Dirty Dre didn't stop running until they got to the end of the hallway. They were laughing and out of breath.

"Damn h-h-hemophiliacs," Dirty Dre said. He was bent over, hands on his knees, trying to catch his breath.

Eric shook his head. "You mean hermaphrodites, dumb ass," he laughed.

"Whatever. I see why they call it the Hall of Surprises," Dirty Dre shot back.

"I thought you liked surprises," Eric teased.

"Hey, guys," a pair of deep voices purred from the darkness.

Eric and Dirty Dre stood still like English pointers. They slowly peeked inside the room where the voices came from. Two beautiful black women were oiled up and looked ready to play wrestling on the world's biggest sectional sofa.

The two guys looked at each other like Shaggy and Scooby-Doo.

"Uh-oh," Eric said.

"I ain't f-f-falling for that shit again," Dirty Dre said. He turned and walked away.

"Wait, Dirty."

"Nah, man. Fuck this freaky-ass shit," he said over his shoulder. "I'll be at the b-b-bar, where I can tell the clits from the d-d-dicks."

"But they're naked," Eric yelled down the hall. Too late. Dirty had turned the corner.

Eric took a step inside the room for a closer inspection.

"Stand up," he ordered.

They obeyed, hands on their ample hips.

"Turn around."

Although they were confused at the order, they obeyed.

"Bend over."

They did.

They're women alright.

Eric stepped inside the room and closed the door.

The room was actually the living room of a mini-apartment. It had the luxurious look of a hotel and a fully stocked bar. The women circled Eric, sizing him up. They were sharks.

"My name is Lava. What's yours, handsome?" said the taller of the two.

Eric gulped. "Um, Eric. H-how did you get a name like Lava?"

She licked her lips. " 'Cause I got the hottest pussy on the planet."

Good God. I should have brought some Viagra.

Lava was at least five foot ten. She was dark skinned, slender, and wore her hair in short braids. Lava looked Eric up and down like he was a piece of meat. He felt cheap.

"Ouch!" Eric jerked around. The other woman had pinched his ass.

"They call me Pacific," she said. She was shorter by an inch and had long straight blonde hair. Brown skinned with a cute cheerleader look, Pacific had the curvy shape of a world-class rump shaker. Her thong was MIA inside her cheeks.

"And wh—?" Eric attempted to say.

" 'Cause I have the wettest and deepest pussy on the planet," she cut him off. Eric wanted his mama. *What in the hell have I gotten myself into?*

"Can I get a rum and Coke? No, make that a double shot of rum and some ice."

"Whatever you want, sweet thang," Lava purred, and stuck her finger in her mouth. "And I mean whatever you want." She smiled like a demon.

Eric tried to hide his fear. *This bitch is the Antichrist.*

Lava walked behind the bar. It was stocked with all the popular brands of liquor. She poured him a drink. Pacific toyed with his zipper.

Oh shit.

She smiled and pulled it down.

"How long do you want to party?" Lava said, pulling out an ice tray.

"Huh?"

He had his eyes on Pacific. She pushed him down onto the couch and knelt down in front of him. She hungrily pulled his pants down.

"I asked how long do you want to party?"

"All night," Eric answered, as his eyes rolled back.

Lava crushed a small tab of Ecstasy and sprinkled it in his drink. She then set out a mirror with at least a gram of cocaine on it. "You did say that you wanted a rum and some coke, right?" she asked with a sly smile.

"Yeah," Eric moaned.

After arranging the coke in five neat lines, she expertly inhaled three of them.

"Um, good." Her ample chest heaved. " 'Cause it's going to be hot and wet all night."

Chapter Eleven

Eden looked at the clock. 5:30 AM.

Where is he?

The morning show had already begun minus one sports anchor. Eric was two hours late for work, and the clock was ticking. If there was one thing that was certain in television, it was that the show would go on. The anchors had to start the show without him. Eden was worried. Eric was never late. She had called his home and cell phone repeatedly and gotten no answer.

I hope he's okay. Today is Friday. Maybe he thought he was off.

It was hard for her to concentrate on the scripts. She had already mispronounced the name of one city and called General Wesley Clark a senator. At first Bryan, the show's executive producer, was mad at Eric's tardiness, then he became worried. He had left three messages for

Eric. Anchors never missed work without at least calling. For Eric's sake, he hoped that he had a good reason and that Karen Hunter, their news director and boss, wasn't watching the show. If she was watching, then Eric's ass would be in deep trouble.

"Any word on Eric?" Eden asked during a commercial break.

"No," Bryan said in her earpiece.

"I am royally fucked." Eric sighed, looking at his watch. He flashed his ID badge and sprinted past Clarence, the long-time ABC security guard.

"Late one, huh?" Clarence asked.

"Too damn late," Eric yelled back to him.

Eric had eight minutes to get up two flights of stairs, change, and get on the set for his next sports segment. He had already missed the first one. His heart was racing.

I hope my scripts are ready. Karen is going to fire me. Coke? I'm so stupid. A nigga ain't gon' never learn.

Eric would have slept right through his segment if Dirty Dre hadn't searched nearly every room at The Goat looking for him. With all of his stuttering, it took him an eternity just to explain who he was looking for. He found Eric passed out between two snoring beauties. The room was a mess. Empty liquor bottles, a half-smoked blunt, and smudges of cocaine were all over the coffee table.

"What the f-f-uck?" Dirty stuttered.

A porno tape, *Weapons of Ass Destruction #2*, was stuck on pause in the VCR. Dirty Dre stared at the screen while he shook and slapped Eric. "W-w-wake up!"

" 'Bout time you got here," said Todd, his sports producer. He held Eric's suit jacket and tie out to him. "You better hurry up. Bryan is pissed."

Eric ignored the comment. "Forget the pants. I'll just wear the jacket."

"But you have on jeans," Todd said, exasperated.

Eric grabbed the scripts and took off running.

"Eric?"

"What?" he snapped.

Todd had a startled look on his face. "Your nose?"

"My what?"

Todd pinched his own nose. The universal you-got-cocaine-all-over-your-nose signal.

"Aw, shit. Thanks, just a little makeup," Eric said, embarrassed. *I can't believe I snorted that shit. I'm slipping real hard.*

Eric made it to the studio with less than a minute to spare. Eden and Ryan stared at him, then eyed each other suspiciously. They thought Eric looked tired and worn out, like he had the flu.

Eric took a deep breath. "Okay, I'm ready."

He shuffled his scripts. They looked blurry. *Damn, I'm still high*, he thought.

Right before Eden was about to toss to him, the floor director gave her the signal for commercial.

Eden didn't skip a beat and tossed to the commercial.

Eric threw up his hands. "What happened?" he snapped.

The floor manager pointed to his shirt. Eric looked down and instantly felt ill.

His nose was bleeding.

"Damn! Damn! Damn!"

Eric, nearly distraught, paced back and forth in his bedroom, cursing and kicking everything in sight.

"How fucking stupid can you be, Eric?" he screamed at an overturned clothes hamper. He threw a pillow at the dresser. The sound of a jewelry box and candles crashing to the floor echoed in his head. The mirror wobbled, warping his reflection.

"You really fucked yourself this time," he yelled before launching a ceramic vase against the wall. It was only 7 AM but Eric was done for the day. Bryan had sent him home sick, but rumors were already running rampant among the floor crew. The cellular phone clipped to his belt vibrated. He ripped it from the case and threw it into the hallway.

"Come on, E. Cocaine? Nose-bleeding on the goddamn set? Aw, man, they gon' think I'm a crackhead," he continued, cursing at himself.

The cordless phone rang. It was the third time in less than half an hour. He answered it. "What?"

Dead air.

"Eric?"

He winced. It was Eden. "Oh, sorry sweetheart. I was asleep," he lied.

"Sorry to wake you. Are you okay?"

"Uh, yeah . . . I'm fine."

"I was worried. You left before the show was over."

"I'm not feeling too well." He picked up an expensive blazer from the floor. He had worn it the night before and wanted to hang it up. There was something crunchy in the breast pocket. He pulled it out. It was a small envelope. *What's this?*

"What happened? Did you hurt yourself?" Eden asked.

"No . . . no . . . it's an old football injury," he lied again, distracted by the small envelope. "I, uh, broke my nose twice and sometimes when my sinuses act up, it bleeds." The envelope was signed "A gift from Lava."

"Your sinuses make your nose bleed?" Eden sounded skeptical.

"Not the sinuses, mainly the blowing of my nose. If I blow it too hard, sometimes it bleeds."

"Oh," she said.

Eric pulled open the flap. *Oh shit, she gave me some coke.*

"You want me to come over?"

He didn't hear Eden. He stared at the cocaine.

"Eric?"

"Sorry, um, I do, but I have a doctor's appointment," he lied for the third time.

"Are we still on for church on Sunday?" she reminded him. "Reverend Francois is preaching."

"I wouldn't miss it for the world," Eric said absently.

"Okay, call me later."

"Bye." He quickly hung up.

Eric rushed to the bathroom. He started to flush the envelope but paused. A little voice in his head said, *Don't flush it, stupid. That's a lot of coke.*

Instead, Eric feverishly dumped it on the counter. The cocaine looked like a sparkling tablespoon of sugar. Eric dipped his index finger in the white pile and rubbed it across his gums. He winced from the bitter taste, but seconds later his gums tingled. Then they went numb.

Damn, this is some good shit. All other thoughts left him. He hurriedly fished a crisp twenty-dollar bill from his pocket. *Oh well, it's Friday. I don't have to go back to work. Might as well get high.*

After tightly rolling the bill into a makeshift straw, he spread out a couple of lines and inhaled them deeply. Thirty seconds later, Eric felt like he had won the lottery. The cocaine made Eric feel as if his vision was telescopic. He had unusual mental clarity and heightened senses, especially his sense of smell and hearing. As he leaned back in his sofa listening to the sounds of Miles Davis, he swore the jazz legend was blowing his trumpet right there in his living room.

Damn, this is some really good coke.

It had to be good if it made him forget what had happened earlier that morning. The drug washed away any feelings of embarrassment or regret. Cocaine could make a normal user feel superconfident. It made Eric feel super-human, invincible.

Fuck them all. I'm Eric mutha-fucking 2 Swift and I'm too swift for them. He laughed.

Eric chopped and divided more of the drug on his glass coffee table, then inhaled another line. The back of his throat tingled, and he couldn't keep his fingers from pinching his nose. Every movement seemed to be blurry yet at the same time crystal clear.

Brring!

Eric stared at the ringing phone. It sounded like a firetruck racing to a scene.

Brring! the ringer echoed.

He reached for it, but his arm was too short. Then he realized that the phone was across the room. He grinned.

Brring!

It took all of his strength to get up and answer it.

"Hellooo," he giggled.

"Yo, E. What up?"

"Who this?"

"LeBaron, stupid. Who does it sound like?"

"Yo mama." Eric fell back laughing onto the sofa. His foot kicked the table and a puff of the white powder fell off the side. His bottle of Corona wobbled.

"Shit."

"What's wrong with you?" LeBaron sounded concerned.

"You know what's my problem, LeBaron? Chrysler LeBaron?" He snickered.

"What . . . Eric? Erica Kane?" LeBaron shot back.

"I'm rich and I'm too goddamn good-looking."

"Are you drunk?"

"You know I don't drink." Eric smirked while taking a sip of the Corona.

"Now I know you're drunk. Look, man, I really need to talk to you about something. It's real important. Phoe—"

"Hold on," he cut him off. "Be quiet for a second, LeBaron." Eric stood and walked over to the front door. He put his ear to the door.

"What's wrong with you?" LeBaron demanded.

"Shh," Eric whispered.

"What is it?" LeBaron was growing frustrated.

Eric remained silent.

"I thought I heard the police at my door." Eric fell back laughing. "Gotta go, bro." The line went dead.

Confused, LeBaron looked at his phone. *What the hell was that about? He sounded high.*

LeBaron rubbed his chin. "I need to go and check on my boy."

Chapter Twelve

Eric, still buzzing from a two-day coke and liquor binge, stared at the ceiling and shook his head for a third time. He couldn't seem to get the ringing in his ears to stop. The main reason he couldn't stop the ringing was because it was the phone that was ringing. He squinted at his clock.

"Nine AM!" he mumbled, and swung his legs over to the side of the bed. "I must've passed out last night." Actually, he had passed out the last two nights in a row.

The phone continued to ring. Eric ignored it. He bent over and put his aching head in his hands. He smacked his lips. "Damn, I'm supposed to go to church with Eden this morning. I don't know how I'm gon' make it."

The phone finally stopped ringing. Eric rubbed his eyes and looked at the caller ID. He had three messages. He picked up the cordless phone and checked the first message, which was from his boss.

"Hello Eric, this is Karen. I'm calling to see if you're okay. Call me on my cell, tonight."

He looked at the date of the message. "Friday?" He rolled his eyes. "Aw, damn, she called me on Friday. Today is Sunday. Where the hell have I been? Karen must be pissed that I didn't call her. I hope she doesn't think I'm doing drugs because of my nose-bleeding. I need to make up a good lie."

He checked the next message.

"Yo, Eric. It's D-D-Dirty," Dre stuttered. "Don't ever take me to no g-g-gay shit like that again."

Eric laughed and thought about The Goat. "Whoa, that was a crazy-ass night."

He checked the next message.

"Eric, it's Eden. Remember, you're picking me up at ten AM sharp. Don't be late."

Eric looked at the clock. "Uh-oh, I better hurry."

New Sunlight Baptist Church was one of the oldest and most respected houses of worship in Harlem. Located in the heart of Striver's Row, it had been a central part of the community for more than eighty years. Black history was literally etched on the walls in a series of beautiful murals depicting momentous events ranging from colored troops being welcomed home from World War I to the Harlem Renaissance to the Civil Rights movement.

"Over there, Eric." Eden pointed to the empty spaces

in a pew close to the front. "I can't believe we have seats this close."

"Great." Eric smiled sarcastically. "I can't believe we're on time, long as I had to wait for you to get from in front of the mirror in the car."

The seats were choice seats indeed, and the church was filling up fast. It was the third Sunday of the month, otherwise known as twenty-somethings Sunday, when the bulk of the congregation would be filled with young people. The main speaker, as usual, would be Reverend Francois, and seating was routinely standing room only. The whole vibe of the church was different on third Sundays. Most of the older members avoided the eleven o'clock service like the plague. "What done got into these young people?" was a phrase often muttered. As parishioners filed inside the church, instead of the soft sounds of an organ, the church's high tech sound system would be thumping Donnie Mc-Clurkin or the latest Yolanda Adams gospel hit. Then the one-hundred-member-strong youth choir would rock the house, setting the stage for the young firebrand, Reverend Francois, who was always sure to give a stirring sermon. It was an ironic scene as the new school clashed with the ancient school. This Sunday was no different. As Eric and Eden settled into their seats, their ears were greeted with a beautiful neosoul rendition of "My Soul Has Been Anchored."

"Thank you, Jesus." Eden raised her hands to the sky and clapped as if she was in a tent revival meeting. Eric glanced at her out of the corner of his eye like she was on crack.

As the choir reached the crescendo, in walked the reverend Joshua Enoch Francois. He was wearing a midnight blue suit with light blue pinstripes. The light and dark blue striped tie he wore looked elegant against the white spread collar dress shirt. He looked like a black Prince Charles. As he walked up the steps to the pulpit, the popular minister waved and acknowledged a few people. He stood motionless with eyes closed until the congregation quieted down.

"Good morning, sisters and brothers, fathers and mothers," he said softly, while adjusting the microphone. The faint screech of feedback could be heard echoing through the rafters. "Today I want to talk about a very controversial topic. The topic is science and religion."

"Science and religion," a parishioner echoed. Reverend Francois nodded.

"Now, most folks with religion don't want any part of science, and most scientists have no use for religion."

A nearby deacon closed his eyes and softly sang, "Well."

Reverend Francois continued. "One side needs proof and all the other side needs is faith. See, I am of the opinion that you can't have one without the other. Can I get an amen?"

"Amen."

"Most preachers are gonna get upset about what I'm

about to say, but I believe that science only reinforces the magnificence of God. As a kid in Sunday school I used to get so confused about the Book of Genesis. You all know the story. God created the world in six days, then rested on the seventh. Like God gets tired. I'm here to tell you that God is in very good shape."

Ripples of giggles could be heard throughout the church.

"What about how God created Adam, Eve, and all the animals? Then so and so begat this one and that one? Blah, blah, blah." The reverend yawned.

The congregation was outright laughing now.

"Pretty standard stuff, right? Definitely simple, but we all grew up on that. See, I've always had issues with that type of teaching. Not that it was wrong or anything, but it was just too simple for me. My conception of God was too big and magnificent for me to accept that. Basically, it wasn't a sophisticated enough explanation for me. You see, I am an intellectual Negro. I'd have to listen to that on Sunday, meanwhile during the week while in science class or in the library, I'm reading about the big bang theory, Charles Darwin's theory of evolution, and archaeological remains of the first humanlike creatures, called hominids, found in Africa one point five million years ago!"

"Preach it," a woman yelled.

"I would constantly ask my Sunday school teacher questions like, 'Where are the dinosaurs in the Bible?' I've been on field trips to the museums and seen the fossils, so

I know they were here. Or, 'If Adam and Eve were the parents of the human race and if they were both white, how did you get black people, brown people, and yellow people out of white people?' Light genes are recessive and even the most basic painter understands that you can't get the color black out of white, but if you mix them right you can get all of the other colors out of black. Ya'll hear me?" He took a step back from the podium. The air inside the New Sunlight was getting electric.

"We hear you, Preacher," the choir echoed.

"And what about the passage 'God created us in his image'? C'mon, now. You mean to tell me that Shabba Ranks or Sam Cassell look like God? I think not."

People were rolling in the pews with laughter and hitting each other on the arms.

"And you mean to tell me that the world, including the Garden of Eden, was created six thousand years ago? The earth is nearly five billion years old and the universe is fifteen billion years old. You know what my Sunday school teacher did? I'ma ask you again. Do you know what my Sunday school teacher did?"

He paused while the congregation asked, "What?"

"She kicked me out of Sunday school. Can you believe that? Kicked me out of Sunday school. I know people in jail who have never been kicked out of Sunday school."

Eric was laughing so hard his eyes were tearing. Reverend Francois unhooked the microphone and stepped down from the pulpit.

"So what did I do? I prayed. I prayed for knowledge, wisdom, and understanding. I prayed for God to unlock the mysteries of the universe. You know what I've learned? I've learned that science only reinforces the magnificence of God. I learned that everything in the entire universe is related. The stars, the moon, planets, solar systems, air, water, soil, the elements, atoms, protons, neutrons, molecules, my heart, and your heart can all be traced back to a single solitary element. Not the Garden of Eden, no disrespect, but it's deeper than that. You see, people try to simplify God. First mistake. God isn't some old white man with a long beard surrounded by little white angels. God is everywhere. God is light. God is night. God is the sun. God is the cosmos. God is water. God is fire. God just *is*. My God can't even be imagined. If your eyes were to see my God, your eyes would explode. If my God breathed life into your lungs, your lungs would vaporize. If my God were to whisper in your ears, your ears would melt. My God's touch is so hot. You know how hot the sun is? Do you?"

Reverend Francois pointed to an elderly man sitting in the front pew. "You, sir. Do you know how hot the sun is?" The man shrugged his shoulders.

"C'mon, guess."

The old man rubbed his chin for a second and blurted out, "Five hundred degrees!"

Reverend Francois burst out laughing. "Brother, it's five hundred degrees in here." The minister then handed him a fan with a picture of Martin Luther King Jr. on one side and a Harlem funeral parlor on the other. The congregation got a kick out of the gesture.

"The core of the sun is sixteen million degrees! That qualifies as hot as hell. We complain when it's in the nineties. And get this, the sun is ninety-three million miles away from the earth. It's so big a million planet earths could fit inside it. In just one second, the sun emits more energy than humans have used in ten thousand years! My God's touch is hotter than that.

"How hot, you ask? I'll give you one more science lesson. One second after the big bang, you know how hot the universe was?" He looked around at his congregation. "I don't know why I'm asking. Ya'll don't know. I'll tell you how hot. The universe was one hundred million trillion trillion degrees! That's five trillion trillion times as hot as the sun. My God's touch is hotter than that."

The congregation was on fire. They were standing in their seats.

"You're clapping, huh? You think you know but you have no idea. All this stuff is basic math for God. What does your God look like? I'll tell you what mine looks like. My God looks like the universe. My God looks like nature. My God is wind. My God is rain. My God is colder than the greatest and iciest glaciers. My God is as solid as the mountainous Alps. My God is deeper than the depths of all of the oceans and seas combined. My God is thunder and lightning and tornadoes. My God is hurricanes and tsunamis all rolled into one! My God is all of that plus a whole lot of other things you can't even pronounce. That's what my God looks like, and we are one infinitesimal speck in this gigantic universe, yet we are a part of it too. That's the image that God made us in."

It was near pandemonium in the church.

"I'm sorry," Reverend Francois said, wiping sweat from his forehead. "Are you tired? I know ya'll want to get home. I'm about to wrap up. Can I have one more minute?"

It was so loud he couldn't even make out what the crowd was saying.

"Fifteen billion years ago the big bang created time as we know it along with chemical elements like hydrogen, nitrogen, and carbon. As the universe cooled, galaxies formed along with solar systems and planets like mother earth. The earth's atmosphere is made out of oxygen, nitrogen, and calcium. I ask you, do you know what the human body is made of? The human body is made up of elements like oxygen, nitrogen, and calcium. We are made of the same elements that have been present since the beginning of time. We are all an intricate part of the universe. The universe is an intricate part of all of us. The very existence of the universe proves the very existence of God."

Eric and Eden were silent as they exited the church. The sun was shining on a beautiful seventy-five-degree Sunday.

Eric sighed, feeling a sense of awe and elation. "I'm blown away," he said.

"Reverend Francois is an incredible minister," Eden said.

"He's definitely given me some things to think about."

Eden turned and faced him. "Like what?"

Eric reached out and held her hand. "Like us."

"What do you mean, us?"

"We've been spending a lot of time together. Lunches, church, not to mention all the time at work. It's almost like we are a couple."

"You know, people are thinking we're dating."

Eric grinned. "That's not a bad rumor."

"Stop that." Eden playfully punched him in the arm.

"Eden, I really feel like God brought us together for a reason."

"Really?" She smiled. "Funny you should say that, because I've been thinking about that too."

"Come here," he said, embracing her. Eric looked deep into her eyes and hungrily kissed her. Eden did not resist.

They were lost in each other for nearly a full minute. The couple didn't even hear the young teenager riding by on a bicycle yell out, "Get a room." It took an elderly couple loudly clearing their throats as they walked by to jolt them back to reality.

"Oh my. I'm so embarrassed," Eden said, blushing.

Eric just stood there with a goofy grin on his face. He looked like a ten-year-old getting a Valentine's Day card from a homeroom crush.

Eden rolled her eyes. "Well, say something."

He reached out his arms and mumbled, "Mama."

"You're so simple." Eden grinned, playfully pushing him away.

"Eden, I am going to be real honest with you. I feel butterflies."

"Mine are more like pterodactyls," she said, rubbing her flat stomach. "So what do we do now?"

Eric cheesed. "Well, as the immortal Ray Charles used to say, 'We gon' let it *do* what it *do*, baby.' "

Chapter Thirteen

"Eden, stay calm," Eric said, adjusting the cordless phone to his ear. It was Monday morning, and he was sitting on his sofa with his feet propped up on the coffee table. "It's just a meeting."

Standing outside the network's headquarters on West Fifty-seventh Street, Eden frowned. "How can I stay calm? The president of the news division wants to see me."

"Baby, it has to be good news."

"How do you know? They could be firing me." She pouted.

"Honey, listen. If they were firing you, he wouldn't do it. He's too high up. Karen would do it."

Eden mulled over his words. "I guess so."

"Besides, you're the best thing ABC has. You're the future. A number one draft pick. You are Eden Alexander. A star. Now the world is about to recognize that fact."

She blushed. "You really think I'm a star?"

"Star? Sweetheart, you're a whole solar system."

"You're so good for me," Eden said, laughing.

"You're about to be big time."

"I'm a big-timer," she joked. "Bye, baby."

As Eric clicked off his phone he sighed and said to himself, "Well, at least one of us is going to hit the big time."

Eric sat back and relaxed on his sofa. He had decided to extend his weekend by calling in sick. It was a good decision, especially since he was still hungover from his coke binge. After his nose-bleeding episode at work, he wanted to make sure that his nostrils were fine.

As the elevator crept higher, so did Eden's blood pressure. It was rare that an anchor from local news was summoned to a meeting with Nathan Hawkins, the president of network news. As she exited on the fifty-first floor, Eden was taken aback by the luxury of the suite of offices. She had to use both of her hands to push open the heavy etched glass door. The maroon carpeting was thick and seemed to melt into the dark mahogany walls. Eden wasn't really up on authentic European art, but she was sure that the pictures gracing the walls weren't prints. Compared to the chaos of the newsroom, the suite had the eerie silence and creepy feel of a mausoleum.

After a brief wait Eden was ushered into Nathan's office. It was the size of a large apartment. Furnished with dark overstuffed leather couches and chairs along with a magnificent oak desk and bookcases, the office had the look of an Ivy League library. The wall-to-wall, floor-to-ceiling windows overlooked a stunning view of Central Park. Eden felt her palms get moist.

"Thanks for coming, Ms. Alexander," Nathan Hawkins said, rising from his desk. His voice was a rich, deep baritone, which matched the man. Standing six foot two with a shock of silver hair and a gruff demeanor, he looked like the father from the eighties televison series *Dallas*. Nathan Hawkins was legendary in the world of broadcasting. He was a no-nonsense former marine who valued discipline and respect. He'd created some of the longest-lasting news programs in history and launched the careers of most of the major network anchors and reporters. A nod from him could change the life of a young anchor.

Eden cleared her dry throat. "The pleasure is mine, Mr. Hawkins."

Nathan pointed at a man sitting on one of the couches. "This gentleman is David Denson, the executive producer of *America This Morning*."

David stood and shook Eden's hand. They sat down, and Nathan got right to the point.

"Ms. Alexander, how would you like to fill in on *America This Morning*?"

Eric prepared his apartment as if he was receiving a royal visitor. The only things missing were a red carpet and brass band. Tonight was a big night, Eden's first and hopefully not last visit to his place. They were supposed to be celebrating her opportunity to anchor the network news. Eric was celebrating for a different opportunity.

Tonight's the night. No more Mr. Nice Guy.

With the Notorious B.I.G. and R. Kelly's "I'm F'ing You Tonight" serving as the sound track, Eric made last minute preparations. He lit the last of the scented candles and placed them strategically on brass stands around his large living room to affect the best lighting. Eric had pushed his sofa set against a back wall and replaced it with huge maroon and gold silk and satin pillows atop two thick Persian carpets. The room looked magical and Middle Eastern, a scene right out of *One Thousand and One Nights.* The intercom buzzed. The concierge was sending Eden up.

Right on time.

As Eric stood behind his bar and refreshed his Rémy and Coke, he surveyed his handiwork. He was impressed. Not bad for an ex-jock.

"You ain't lying, R. Kelly." Eric hummed. "I'm sexin' Eden tonight." He then quickly replaced the CD with Barry White singing "Secret Garden," just in time for the doorbell to ring.

The Garden of Eden won't be a secret after tonight.

Eden was glowing. She wore a sleeveless pink and tan Victoria's Secret dress with matching pink and tan Coach sandals and purse.

I hope everything's pink and tan, Eric thought.

A one-carat diamond pendant and earring set rounded out her ensemble. Eric could only stare.

"What's wrong?" Eden stood there with her hands on her slender hips.

He reached out and took one of her hands, gently squeezing it. "Words cannot properly describe how magnificent you look, Eden." Eric was sincere. "Someone should write a song about you."

She blushed. "Thank you, Mr. Swift. You look quite dapper yourself."

Eric felt quite dapper too. He had on a long-sleeved light blue silk shirt and midnight blue slacks. His black alligator shoes and matching belt glistened. They shone almost as bright as his platinum Cartier watch.

"Your place is fantastic," Eden admired. "I love what you've done with it."

He pulled her close. "I bought all of this just for tonight," he joked. "It's going back after you leave in the morning."

She smirked. "What makes you think I'll be here in the morning?" She playfully pushed him away. Eric kissed her deeply.

Keep this up and I might not ever leave, Eden thought when Eric released her from his embrace.

While Eric poured her a drink, she scanned his large library of books, impressed. "You and your books. You have quite a diverse collection. Have you read them all?"

"Some twice," he said, handing her a chilled glass of Pinot Grigio. He gave her a tour of his library. "Over here are my spiritual books, the Bible, the Torah, the Koran, and, oh, here's one of my favorites . . . *Science and God*." Eric sounded like a little boy telling his parents about some amazing accomplishment.

Eden pulled a volume from the shelf. "Hmm . . . *The Art of Seduction?* And what's this? *How to Have Success with Women*."

"Research," he joked. He grabbed them from her hand and hastily put them back on the shelf.

She reached around him. "Oh, and what about these? *How to Make Anyone Fall in Love with You* and *What Women Want?*"

Eric had a sheepish grin on his face.

"And tell me, Professor Swift," Eden asked, as if she was interviewing him on the morning show, "what do women really want?"

"Everything," he deadpanned.

Minutes later they were settled on the pillows, laughing and eating shrimp cocktail.

"You are going to be such a big star," Eric said.

"I can't wait," she giggled.

Eden felt light-headed but safe in Eric's arms. For weeks she had longed to be with him, but he made her nervous. Eden was used to totally dominating everything and everyone in her universe. It was obvious that Eric wasn't one to be dominated, at least not easily.

"Turn that up." Eden snapped her fingers. "I haven't heard Atlantic Starr in years."

Eric pulled Eden to her feet and they slow-danced. While he held on to her waist like it was a ledge, he softly sang in her ear.

"Ooh, you have a wonderful voice," Eden purred.

A wonderful voice? I gotcha now.

Eric had trained his voice in several years of high school and college choirs. His father played a mean guitar and his mother sang lead in the church choir, so music had been a constant in his life. Eric loved to spring his voice on women. It never failed. It was his weapon of ass destruction.

"You know something, Eden?" He nibbled on her earlobe.

She arched her neck as the pleasure rolled over her. He continued slowly, making sure he got the words just right. Eric had practiced what he was about to say for at least an hour.

"Holding you right now, I realize that paradise is true and all of God's angels must look just like you."

Eden giggled like a schoolgirl. "Ooh, Eric . . . I didn't know you were a poet too."

He continued. "Every time you spread your wings, heaven's choir starts to sing."

Eden held him tighter.

"And it sounds so sweet to me. Woman, I'll love you for an eternity.

"In you, I see the brilliance of God and the beauty of humanity. You are majestic, and my reason for living is to celebrate your vanity. Eden, you are as complex as the universe yet simple like the changing of the seasons. I can't count the ways that I love you nor explain my many reasons."

Eden kissed his neck.

"Your emotions run deeper than oceans, a temperament that rages like stormy seas. Your fury erupts like a fiery volcano; it's brought peace to empires, and nations to their knees."

Eric squeezed her tight. She held him closer.

"You are balance, order. Inside you germinates the seed of life. And the gentleness of your touch eases all my pain, all my strife. Letting me know that when blue skies turn gray or light fades to dark and my tortured soul lies worn and beaten, I can rest my weary head upon your loving heart and listen to the echoes of Eden."

Eden kissed Eric long and deeply as tears ran down her face. "That was so beautiful," she sobbed.

"Baby, are you sad?" Eric held her face in his hands.

"I'm far from sad." Eden pulled away from him and felt her face. "Oh my goodness, look at me. I must be a mess."

"You look fantastic," Eric said.

"I'll be right back. Let me get my face together." She smiled and ran her hand across Eric's growing bulge. "Then we can pick up where we left off."

By the time Eden had closed the bathroom door, Eric was in his Jockeys.

"I'm . . . fucking you . . . tonight," he sang under his breath.

Eden looked around the spacious bathroom for a Kleenex. She noted that the bathroom was impressive, all cream and tan marble. *He's a man. I bet he doesn't have any tissue other than toilet tissue*, she thought.

Eden opened the bottom cabinet. Nothing. *I wonder if he has any in his medicine cabinet. I shouldn't open his medicine cabinet, though, should I?*

She did.

"Hmm, let's see. Toothpaste, Issey Miyake . . . that's why he always smells so nice. Um . . . what's this? Enzyte? That's good, he takes vitamins."

Eden paused. *Why does he have a rolled-up twenty-dollar bill in his medicine cabinet?*

After seeing what was beside it, she understood.

"Oh my God. Is that cocaine?" Eden nearly knocked over a bottle of Jergens in her state of panic. Her mind flashed back to all of their dates. She thought about how overly funny and hyped Eric always seemed to be.

As a reporter, Eden had investigated stories on drugs and knew one of the biggest signs of cocaine use was a bleeding nose. The drug ate away at the lining of the nostrils. She wondered how she could have missed the signs. Eden also knew the long history that cocaine had in the media industry. Countless anchors and reporters had been destroyed by the substance. She imagined the headlines in the *New York Post:* "Morning Show Anchors

Nabbed in Coke Bust" along with pictures of her and Eric.

No way, she thought. She had too much to lose. In a few days she was going to anchor a network show. Nothing and no one would stand in her way.

Eden closed the medicine cabinet and stormed out of the bathroom. Eric was on the couch in his underwear, singing. Eden ignored him, picked up her purse, and put her shoes on.

"Hey, where you going?" he nervously asked.

"Sorry, I have to leave." Eden turned and started for the door.

Eric raced to the door, positioning himself between it and her. "What's wrong? What happened?"

"Nothing, really . . ." She searched for a lie, something she wasn't used to doing. Unconvincingly, she said, "This isn't right. I'm not ready for all this."

"Huh? But—" Eric was dumbfounded.

She cut him off. "Can you please move?" Eden couldn't get out of his place fast enough. Irrationally, she was sure that agents from the DEA were on the way to take them both to jail. Her reputation had to come before any relationship, no matter how delicious it might promise to be.

Eric stepped aside.

Eden walked through the door without saying goodbye.

Eric stood there stunned and feeling really limp.

Chapter Fourteen

"I get an office just so that I can prep for the show?" Eden said in amazement to the production assistant who opened the door to a spacious dressing room.

"Yes, Ms. Alexander," the PA said. "All of the anchors have an office."

"All of the 'anchors' have one? But I'm just filling in." Anchor, huh? She liked the sound of that. An enormous smile crossed Eden's face as she gazed out the large window. The spare office had a great view of Central Park. She couldn't get over the fact that though she was just a fill-in, she had the use of a luxurious office, complete with her own restroom. At the local station where she was a main anchor, Eden didn't even rate a cubicle, just a desk. "Susan better watch out. I can get used to this."

The PA laughed. Susan LaFontaine was the weekend show's main anchor for the network. She'd just had a baby and was determined to take as much time as the government allowed. As Eden settled in, a small army of producers and assistants raced in and out of the office bringing her scripts, rundowns, and research information. The whirl of activity was dizzying.

God, she prayed. *Please give me the strength*.

And if that wasn't overwhelming enough, Eden was constantly being called to the studio to go over her stage marks, lighting, and for rehearsals. She had to endure all of this while two high-priced makeup artists and one hairstylist primped and prodded her. She felt like a runway model. The network had even given her a clothing allowance to buy new clothes. Eden had spent five thousand dollars and an entire afternoon getting fitted at Saks Fifth Avenue and loved every minute.

This was a long way from her first job as a weekend reporter in Beaumont, Texas, market 212. There, Eden had to film, edit, and voice her own stories. Even then she hungered for the big time. No story was too small or dirty for her to report. She got drenched in hurricanes, nearly succumbed to smoke inhalation reporting on house fires, reported on serial killers, sexual predators, and kidnappings. The daily grind and deadlines hardened her. The lifestyle also deprived her of a stable relationship, a fact of life for most ambitous reporters and anchors. Eden was one of the most ambitious.

It normally took a reporter three to five years just to move up a few notches in market size. Eden made the jump to weekend anchor in Tulsa market 56 in two years. From there she spent two years in Detroit, market 12, before getting the call to come to broadcasting's promised land, New York, market 1.

Now Eden was on the cusp of anchoring a national network show, a chance that only a handful of broadcasters ever got. She was determined to make the most of her opportunity. As she made her way to the set, the hair and makeup artists buzzing around her like flies, Eden said another silent prayer.

She would need it. The next hour would change her life forever.

"Eden?" said a disembodied voice in her ear.

She ignored the voice. She was too busy reading scripts. The show was going to begin in three minutes.

"Eden, can you hear me?"

She jerked around, then slowly put her finger on her earpiece and said, "Yes."

"I need you to listen real close to what I am about to tell you." It was David Denson, the weekend morning show's executive producer.

"I'm listening." Her heart was starting to beat rapidly.

"On the way to the studio Richard slipped and fell and hit his head." Richard Roberts was the morning show coanchor.

Eden swallowed hard. "Is he alright?" she asked.

"His face is pretty swollen, but he should be okay. I'm sending him to the emergency room as a precaution."

"Okay. Who is going to coanchor?"

"You are going to go solo," David said. "Okay?"

Her options were fight, flight, or freeze. Eden chose the latter, or rather, her body made the decision for her. She was completely stunned.

"Eden?" he repeated.

After a second Eden blinked and said, "Absolutely." Her pulse began racing and her insides turned to oatmeal.

She'd been relying on Richard, who had years of network experience, to carry most of the load. Eden would focus mainly on the voice-overs and tossing to reporters. She would have to get up to speed on his segments on the fly and during commerical breaks.

"Oh my Lord," she whispered when a new fact came to her attention. Richard was going to interview the homeland security advisor! "Breathe," she told herself, reaching for Richard's stack of scripts.

The show's opening music started. Eden thought she might hyperventilate. *Pull it together, girl. God wouldn't bring you this far for you to fail.*

The camera opened to a wide sweeping shot of Eden sitting alone behind the large anchor desk before tightening to a close-up.

"Good morning and thank you for joining ABC's *America This Morning Weekend Edition*. I'm Eden Alexander, in for Susan LaFontaine and Richard Roberts. Our top story this morning: The nation's terror alert has been upgraded to orange. We're joined today by the head of the Department of Homeland Security, Secretary William Howell."

Do I call him Mr. Secretary? "Thanks for joining us, Mr. Secretary."

"My pleasure, Eden."

He knows my name?

"Secretary Howell, what prompted this sudden upgrade?"

As the secretary answered, Eden furiously tried to read the next question and some background information while at the same time attempting to listen to his answer.

"Mr. Secretary, I think the American people feel like yo-yos because—uh, I believe we have a graphic, can we put that up? There it is. Your office said just four days ago the threat was at best minuscule. Now we're at orange?"

Damn, where did that come from? Eden thought, surprised at what had come out of her mouth. She nevertheless sat there with a stern look on her face.

The secretary stuttered, taken aback. When informed he would be interviewed by Eden, the secretary had figured it would be a softball interview. He stumbled for an answer but came off unprepared. Inside the control room David Denson was impressed. He said aloud to no one in particular, "Folks, I think we found ourselves a winner."

Chapter Fifteen

Eric's nose tingled and he was still sniffling from the three lines of cocaine he had just snorted in the newsroom's bathroom. The drug exacerbated the anger he was still feeling from the previous night with Eden. Earlier that morning he'd expected to see her, but she wasn't at work. He was pissed when Bryan announced that Eden would be on leave from the show while filling in on the network. That meant she was off the show and effectively out of his life. He was hoping to speak with her about what had happened. He had called Eden all weekend but got no response. He'd left five messages. Eric wasn't used to being dumped. As he waited for his sports segment his mind drifted.

Fuck it and fuck her. I don't have time for these silly-ass games.

"Four-three-two-one," the floor director counted out to Eric.

The camera cut to him and caught him looking off to the side, smirking.

Damn, I didn't even get to hit that.

The floor director waved furiously for him to start reading. Eric's mind was in another time zone. He sat there, oblivious, thinking about how Eden had stormed out on him and half distracted by a monitor tuned to a competing station. It was on the bawdy WB network's morning show. It was airing a segment featuring bikini-clad models. "Goddammit, go, Eric!" the producer screamed into his earpiece.

"Huh?" Eric jerked toward the camera. "Oh shit! I'm on? Uh-oh, oh God. I'm sorry." Eric covered his mouth with his hand as if that would take the gaffe back. The other anchors and the floor crew were stunned.

"Go to commercial! Go to commercial!" the producer screamed.

Eric sat across from Karen, the station's news director, his mouth dry and beads of sweat glistening on his forehead. He had trouble focusing.

"You fucked up," she said. Her stare was icy. Eric sat there silent.

Karen was a no-nonsense kind of boss and accepted nothing less than the highest level of performance from her employees, especially high-priced anchors.

"Let me ex—"

"Shut up," she yelled. "There is no acceptable explanation for what you did yesterday morning. You embarrassed yourself, your colleagues, and more important, this station. I am so pissed at you."

Karen was livid. She had been at a media conference in Philadelphia when she heard the news and rushed back a day early to meet with Eric. The newsroom watched the drama unfold through Karen's large glass office windows. High-priced anchor versus the news director. Who would win? The money was on Karen. Eric looked at the floor and sighed. He hadn't felt this bad since the Washington Redskins cut him.

"Lately your performance has been erratic and sloppy. You haven't broken a big story since you've been here. Plus you look like shit." She eyed him hard. "Is there something you want to tell me?"

Yeah, fuck off, he thought. He shook his head no.

"I'm going to be frank with you, Eric. I want to fire you, but the general manager won't let me, so I am going to suspend you indefinitely until you can get your shit together."

Eric's eyes bugged. He'd expected to get an ass-chewing but not this. "What? Suspend me? For a little mistake?" He started to rise from the chair.

She waved a copy of the sports section of the *New York Post* at him. He sat back down. "See this caption? *'Eric's Not Too Swift!'* I'd say that was more than a little mistake." Karen frowned. "I want my anchors to read the headlines, not make them."

"Karen."

"Eric, this isn't up for discussion. Good-bye." She put on her reading glasses and looked down at some paperwork.

Eric continued to sit there, stunned. *I should never have snorted that coke.*

Karen looked up. "You're still here."

"How can you be so cold?"

"It's easy when the screwup is of this magnitude," she said matter-of-factly.

"What about second chances?" Eric asked.

"I haven't fired you yet. So there's your second chance."

The last time Eric had cried, he was ten years old. It was his first day of Pop Warner football practice, and he was playing running back. An older boy tackled him hard, and after the play he asked the coach to take him out of the game. The other boys laughed at him. As Eric limped to the sideline crying, his father pulled him aside and whispered what was to become Eric's mantra.

"Son, when you get hit hard, hit back harder."

Eric had never been hit harder than he had been today. As he left Karen's office, the stares of the other people in the newsroom were almost too much to take. They reminded him of the little boys who had made fun of him. Eric held on and ignored the stares and whispers. He wouldn't cry, at least not in front of them.

When he got home it was a different story. Even a full glass of cognac couldn't keep the tears from streaming down his face. He felt disgraced. Eric thought about calling his father, but this would kill him. He was glad that his parents lived in Atlanta. At least they wouldn't have to read in the New York papers how their son shamed the family.

"You are one stupid motherfucker!" Eric threw the glass at the fireplace. Shards of glass exploded in all directions. "How could you do it?" He and his apartment were a wreck.

"No, no, no," he mumbled, his face in his hands. "This is not happening to me."

He grabbed the bottle of cognac and took a deep gulp. "Ahh shit!" The warm liquid burned his chest. He wiped the beads of sweat from his forehead.

"What am I going to do?"

Eric thought about all the things he needed to do at a time like this. He could pray, call his parents or LeBaron. Or call Eden.

Instead, he went into the kitchen and pulled down a mahogany box from on top of the refrigerator. Inside was a quarter kilo of cocaine, about five thousand dollars' worth of drugs. Everything Eric did was big. He broke off a chunk and began mashing it through a flour strainer onto a hand mirror. As the cocaine sifted, it fell onto the mirror in fine grains. Eric went back into the living room and put the coke on the coffee table next to the cognac bottle. He arranged a large portion of the drug into ten fat lines.

Kneeling down, he put the straw to his nostril. He looked like Al Pacino in the gangster classic *Scarface*.

"Oh shit, hold on a minute, Mr. Swift." He grinned. It was a sinister grin.

Eric walked over to his music cabinet. It was a huge cherrywood piece filled with more than two thousand CDs, all arranged by genre and alphabet. He scanned the rows of jazz, classic R & B, and hip-hop. He needed the proper sound track to match his mood.

"Hmm . . . let's see. There you go."

It was the Notorious B.I.G.'s classic album, *Ready to Die*.

Chapter Sixteen

Eden sat, alone and depressed, on the couch in her East Side apartment thumbing through the newspaper's TV sections.

"Dang," she sighed. "I've looked through two papers and none of them wrote about me."

Eden's performance on the weekend show had been excellent; everybody told her so, including David Denson. He told her that if she kept it up he would consider hiring her full-time, although he didn't know in what capacity. Eden knew exactly what capacity she wanted: weekend anchor.

Eden's phone rang. She hoped it wasn't Eric. He had called her so much in the past week that she was thinking of changing her phone number. She didn't have time for coke fiends. She smiled when she saw the caller ID. It was her mother, Alycia.

"Hey, Mom."

Before Eden could get in another word, her mother cut her off. "You were absolutely wonderful, baby," Alycia gushed. "Your father and I are so proud of you. You know everybody was at the house watching."

"What?" Eden yelped. "Mother, it was a news show, not the Super Bowl."

"It was the Super Bowl for us. You should have seen your uncle Winston. He was acting a natural-born fool after you interviewed the gentleman from the homeland defense."

"That's my favorite uncle." Eden howled with laughter.

Alycia and Eden's father, Jacob, lived just outside of Washington, D.C., in the affluent suburb of Fairfax, Virginia. Both successful corporate lawyers, they had instilled in their only daughter a strong sense of achievement. Like most successful parents, they had wanted her to follow in their footsteps or to become a doctor. But Eden wanted to be on television. As a child she would watch newscasts for hours. It didn't matter if it was the local or network news. She didn't watch so much for the news but for how the women dressed or carried themselves.

She was particularly impressed with Carol Simpson, the former weekend anchor for ABC. Eden was enthralled with her sense of style and elocution and with the fact that she was an African American woman. One day Carol spoke at a journalism symposium at Howard University. After the discussion, Eden nearly knocked Carol down trying to get to her. She peppered her idol with nearly a dozen questions before a professor had to literally pull Carol away. Eden was unfazed. She knew what she wanted to be, a network anchor.

"Mother, you really think I did okay?" Eden said. She sounded like a little girl. Like most anchors, she needed approval.

"Sweetheart, you were magnificent. Didn't you read the *Daily News*?"

"Huh? Mama, what are you talking about?"

"Eden, you know that I was going to look at every newspaper to see if they wrote about my baby."

"They don't have the *Daily News* in Virginia." Eden sounded confused.

"I read it online in the TV section."

Eden frantically searched the papers she had on the couch. "But I looked—"

Alycia cut her off. "I'm telling you, Eden, I read it."

Eden ignored her. She rummaged through the *New York Times*, the *Post*. "There it is," she said triumphantly. "I haven't read the *Daily News* yet."

Eden furiously flipped the pages to the TV section. Her picture was on the bottom of the front page of the section. The headline read "Dynamic Debut for New Anchor."

Eden screamed in delight and danced in place.

Her euphoria was immediately cut short when she saw who was on the top half of the section. It was a picture of

Eric under a caption that read "Sports Anchor Suspended."

"Oh my God!" Eden exhaled. It was like she had been punched in the stomach.

"I told you it was a great review, baby," Alycia said.

Eden was silent.

"Eden?" Alycia asked. "What's wrong, sweetheart?"

"Mama, I have to go." Eden clicked off the phone.

Chapter Seventeen

For many people in local television news, the only thing
more interesting than breaking news is breaking gossip.
Hot gossip is a force that can drive decisions ranging from
news coverage to career moves. The broadcast television
gossip wire is a complex network made up of media writers,
disgruntled employees, industry rumors, and hundreds of
Internet sites. Two of the most popular are TVSPY and
NewsBlues.com. These websites consist of the latest hap-
penings in newsrooms all over the country. Fueled by
sources in various newsrooms, the sites keep their fingers
on the pulse of the industry. And the pulse was always racing in newsrooms. The Internet sites were required reading for most news veterans.

LeBaron was no different. After reading at least four
newspapers, he normally began his morning with a cursory
look at these sites. As he scrolled through the listings of

firings and scandals, he froze at a posting marked "New York Sports Anchor Suspended."

"Hmm . . . I wonder who fucked up this time." He clicked on the headline.

"Eric?" LeBaron yelled. A few startled people in the newsroom glanced at his office. LeBaron felt weak.

Huh? He cursed on air? LeBaron kept reading.

Nosebleeds? Suspected drug use? That's crazy.

LeBaron was stunned and couldn't believe what he was reading. Then he remembered how weird Eric had acted during their last conversation. He reached for the phone and dialed Eric.

Pick up, he silently urged.

No answer. He dialed Eric's cell phone number. Eric always kept his cell on. It rang seven times. As LeBaron was about to hang up, Eric answered. He was full of jokes . . . or full of something.

"Who the fuck is this? Calling me at seven forty-six in the morning, crack of dawning?" he groggily imitated the famous rap from the Notorious B.I.G's classic song "Warning."

"Ain't no time for jokes. What the fuck is going on with you?" LeBaron was pissed.

"You tell me, nigga. You're the one blowing my phone the fuck up."

"Are you high?" LeBaron demanded. "Huh? Tell me."

Eric was taken aback. "Yo, you must be out your damn mind, screaming on me. I ain't your bitch."

LeBaron ignored him. "Yo, E, what's this shit I'm reading about you online? You got suspended for drugs?"

"Aw, shit." Eric snapped wide awake. "Where did you read that?"

"NewsBlues, where else? And they got it from the *Daily News*."

Eric cleared his throat. "Some minor drama at the station. A misunderstanding."

LeBaron pulled the phone away from his ear and looked at it in amazement. "E, I'm not a naive intern. You expect me to believe that bullshit?"

Eric paused. "I don't give a flying fuck what you believe. It's my business."

LeBaron felt like he was talking to a total stranger. "Eric, you need some help."

"No, what I need is for people to leave me the hell alone."

"Nigga, I ain't people," LeBaron yelled.

"Well, your name damn sure ain't Mr. Swift, so stay the fuck out of my business."

"Oh, it's like that?"

"As Run-D.M.C. said, 'Nigga, it's like that.' "

The line went dead.

LeBaron stared at the phone. "This nigga has lost his mind."

He decided it was time for him to take a trip to New York.

* * *

Later that afternoon LeBaron fought through rush-hour traffic halfway across town to bring Phoenix her favorite sandwich from Quizno's. The Southwest Chicken and Monterey sandwich felt like it weighed a pound. As he prepared and placed the tray of food in front of his pregnant wife, he told her about Eric's troubles.

"Quit playing around, LeBaron. I'm not in the mood." Phoenix squirmed, trying to reposition herself. "My back aches."

And you're making my head ache, LeBaron thought. "Baby, I swear I'm not. I read it online." He adjusted Phoenix's pillow. "He was suspended for drugs. Can you believe it?"

Nonplussed, she flicked the remote. It was time for *Oprah*. "Well, I'm not surprised. Eric was always out there. I bet he was high when he lived here."

Huh? LeBaron thought. *Sometimes I just want to choke the shit out of you*. Instead, he walked across the spacious bedroom and sat down in an overstuffed leather chair. "You've never liked Eric much, huh?" he asked, one eyebrow raised suspiciously.

Phoenix stared at the televison, not bothering to look at him. "That's a stupid thing to say. Eric is like family, but he's spoiled, immature, and has no respect for the women he dates. But, then again, I guess when the women don't have respect for themselves, how can he?"

LeBaron sighed and twirled the small throw pillow between his fingers. "I can't argue with you on that one, but he's my friend and I can't stand by and watch him throw his life away."

Phoenix snapped her head in LeBaron's direction. "LeBaron, Eric's a grown-ass man. What are you going to do? He lives all the way in New York." Her eyes bored into him.

Silence.

Okay, here she goes. She's gonna flip out and tell me that I'm not going to New York.

"Oh no, mister. You're not going to New York."

LeBaron exploded. "What? How are you going to tell me what I'm not gon' do?"

Phoenix struggled to prop herself up on the pillows. "Because I'm your damn wife, that's how."

LeBaron rolled his eyes. "My wife yes, not my fucking warden."

"LeBaron, I'm pregnant and sick to boot and you're telling me that you are going to leave your sick wife to go to New York for another man? What? Are you fucking Eric?"

He was out of the chair in a flash, eyes bugging. "Woman, you must be out of your fucking mind. Why do you always twist shit around like that?" He walked to the window and stared out into the backyard. "You know damn well, Phoenix, that's not the case. I'm only talking about going for one fucking day. Bridgitte can stay with you for a damn day. She's here every night anyway. Are you fucking her?"

Phoenix started crying.

"Quit trying to make me feel guilty. That's such bullshit."

Oh God, here she goes . . . Niagara fucking Falls.

"No, LeBaron, what you're doing is bullshit. You're probably lying. You probably just want to go up there and go to a fucking strip club with that nigga. Since I've been pregnant we don't even have sex like we used to."

"That's because the doctor said if we have sex like we used to we might kill the damn baby! What does our sex life have to do with anything?" he yelled. "This is my fucking friend we're talking about and he needs my help." LeBaron threw up his hands. "Forget it, Phoenix. You win. You're right. You don't need any more stress," he said, storming out of the room.

"LeBaron?" she yelled.

"What?" he yelled from the other room.

"Can you bring me my bag of barbecue chips from on top of the refrigerator?"

I hope you choke on them damn chips, he thought.

"Girl, what's wrong with you? The honeymooners fighting again?" Bridgitte asked while nibbling on Phoenix's leftovers. Phoenix had summoned her girlfriend minutes after her fight with LeBaron.

Phoenix rubbed her belly. "Girl, I thought having a baby was supposed to bring a couple closer."

Bridgitte turned up the empty bag of chips and frowned. "All couples go through that."

Phoenix cocked her head and looked at the door. LeBaron was downstairs watching television. "Guess what LeBaron wants to do?" she whispered.

"What?" Bridgitte leaned in closer.

"He wants to go to New York to visit Eric."

"And?" Bridgitte smirked. "Why do you have to whisper that?"

"You don't see the problem?" Phoenix asked.

Bridgitte rolled her eyes. "Nope."

Phoenix shook her head in disbelief. "Hello?" She pointed to her belly. "I'm pregnant and in danger of losing the baby."

"Well, how long does he want to go for?"

"A day or two."

"Girl, I can stay with you. Let the man go. He probably needs a vacation. If I was married to you, I know I would."

Phoenix frowned. "He ain't taking a vacation. He's on a mission of mercy."

"Huh? What does that mean?"

"Eric just got fired or suspended, something like that."

Bridgitte jumped off the bed. "What? Girl, get outta here. What did he do?"

"Drugs."

"What?" Bridgitte was shocked. "That's crazy."

"Uh-huh. LeBaron says he's on cocaine."

"What?"

"What! What! What! Girl, is that all you can say?" Phoenix snapped.

Bridgitte threw up her hands. "Chill, I'm sorry. I'm just tripping."

Phoenix shrugged her shoulders. "I don't know why you're surprised. You know Eric is grimy."

"I know he's a ho but damn, cocaine? I never figured him to be a crackhead."

"You never know what people do behind closed doors," Phoenix said.

"Well, that settles it," Bridgitte said.

"See, now you understand?"

"I'll be back." Bridgitte headed for the door.

"Where are you going?" Phoenix said.

"To tell LeBaron that I'm going to stay with you while he's in New York."

"Huh? No you're not. You better get back here."

"LeBaron?" Bridgitte yelled.

"Bridgitte, shut up." Phoenix tried to get out of the bed but was too tired.

"Phoenix, stay in the bed." Bridgitte walked over and sat beside her friend. "Look, you can't let the man leave his boy hanging like that. That's not right."

Phoenix lay in bed pouting with her arms folded.

Bridgitte laughed. "That only works on men."

Phoenix flipped her the bird.

Chapter Eighteen

Brrring! Brrring!

"Huh, what?" Eric's phone jolted him out of a deep sleep. The sleep was made even deeper by the liquor and weed he'd had the night before. He couldn't remember where he began the night but he knew for sure he'd ended it at Compass, a hot new bistro less than three blocks from his apartment. Looking at the beautiful blonde woman softly sleeping next to him, he struggled to place where he'd picked her up.

Ah, the bartender. What's her name? Uh . . . yeah, Sydney.

Brring! Brring!

Eric fumbled for the phone. "Um, hello," he whispered, still groggy. He looked at the clock. It was 7 AM.

"Hello, Eric. It's Eden."

The sound of her sweet voice instantly woke him up.

He glanced at Sydney, who had stirred slightly but was still asleep.

"Well, hello, stranger," Eric said, jumping out of bed. "How are you?"

"I'm doing great," Eden said. "But I should be asking you that."

Shit! That's what she's calling about?

"Hold on a moment," he said, cupping his hand over the phone. Eric looked at Sydney again, who was still sleeping. Better yet, she was softly snoring. He tiptoed out of the bedroom and went downstairs into the living room.

"Baby, I missed you," he said. "What happened? Why did you leave like that and why haven't you called?"

"I'm going through some things and with the whole network thing I'm just kind of stressed out."

"I saw. You've been doing a great job. But I thought we were cool."

"Eric, it's not you. It's me."

Not the "it's me not you" bullshit? "C'mon, Eden. Don't give me that. That sounds like the brush-off."

"Eric, I don't want to talk about that right now. I'm calling as a friend to find out how you're doing, given the circumstances."

"So you heard what happened?"

"Of course I did. Everybody has. I read about it in the paper."

"It's bullshit. Bryan has been out to get me since I started at ABC. He never liked me or my style."

Eden rolled her eyes. "But, Eric, people are saying that you are doing drugs."

"C'mon on, Eden. Drugs? You know me. Do I act like I'm on drugs?"

Hello! I saw them in your medicine cabinet, Eden thought. "It doesn't matter what I think, Eric. Apparently other people do."

"Eden, I need to see you. I'm going through a rough time and I need you in my life. When can I see you again? As you well know, I have plenty of free time right now," he joked.

"Eric." Eden sighed. "Look, we are just too different and, to be honest with you, I don't think I can trust you."

"Who are you going to believe, me or a bunch of bullshit rumors?"

"Can you honestly say that you have never lied to me, Eric?"

"Absolutely, I swear," he lied.

"You don't do drugs?" Eden sounded like a prosecutor. "What about other women?"

Eric glanced at his coffee table, where a small pile of cocaine sat on a mirror. There was also a hot pink thong hanging off the couch.

"Hell, no," Eric lied again.

Eden frowned. "Really? Well, Eric, I have something to share with you." Eden started to say more but was cut off by a voice in the background.

"Eric?" a very naked Sydney yelled from the top of the stairs. "Have you seen my panties?"

Aw, fuck! he thought.

He slapped the phone in his hand and shot a death stare at Syndey while saying, "Eden, I can expl— Hello, Eden?"

The response was a click followed by a dial tone.

Chapter Nineteen

The lobby of Trump Place looked like an ancient Roman palace. The luxury high-rise, located on Manhattan's West Side, overlooked the Hudson River. LeBaron marveled at the four marble columns framing a gigantic oak concierge desk. Large couches and chairs were positioned near the huge windows. Blasts of sunlight made the numerous and wonderfully scented freshly cut floral arrangements glow with color. The building had doormen, uniformed security, and a concierge.

Damn, Eric is living large, he thought.

When he walked inside Eric's apartment, the view nearly took LeBaron's breath away. Large floor-to-ceiling windows revealed Manhattan's skyline along with a fantastic view of the Hudson River. He gave Eric a hug and a pound.

"Damn, black man," LeBaron said, dropping his

overnight bag on the hardwood floor. "You done moved up like George Jefferson in this mug."

"It's alright," a scraggly-looking Eric said as he closed the door.

LeBaron walked over to the window and took in the view. "Alright my ass. This is the hottest apartment I've ever seen."

Eric laughed. "Thirty-five hundred dollars a month. Shit better be."

"Enough with the small talk. You know why I'm here, right, E?" LeBaron said as he sat in a leather recliner.

"Phoenix kicked you out?" Eric shot back.

"I wish," LeBaron joked. "This pregnancy shit is killing me."

"I warned you," Eric said from behind the bar. He poured himself a Rémy on the rocks and one with Coke for LeBaron.

"Whatever. But that's not why I'm here."

Eric handed him the drink. "LeBaron, if you're here for one of those bullshit interventions, you could've saved your train ticket and bought a new baby stroller, 'cause I'm straight."

"Eric. Look at what's happened to you. You lost your job."

"Suspended," he snapped.

"You and I know what suspended means in television," LeBaron said.

"Fuck ABC. I'm still rich. I got a couple of mil in the

bank and they still got to pay me my contract, so I'm good."

"What about your reputation?"

"What reputation? I'm sick of this rat race anyway. Smiling and Uncle Tomming for the camera. I'm glad they suspended me."

"Quit lying. What are you gon' do now? Just lay around here and snort coke?"

Eric jerked his head. "What the fuck you mean?"

"I didn't stutter," LeBaron said. "C'mon, E, everybody knows. It's all over the Internet and the newspapers. I'm disappointed in you, man."

Eric slammed his drink down on the bar counter. "Do you think I care if you are disappointed in me? Who are you to talk about me? I am a grown-ass man."

"Shit, when I was all messed up last year over Phoenix, you were at my door telling me about myself."

Eric folded his arms. "So."

"So? That's all you have to say?"

"Look, LeBaron, that was your fucked-up life. I'm cool about my situation so you shouldn't give a shit either."

LeBaron was stunned. He and Eric had disagreements before, but he had never spoken to him like that.

"Eric, you need help."

"No, I need for you and everybody to stay the hell out of my life. What are you here for anyway? Your wife is pregnant. You should be home with her and not up here on some ol' 'Captain Save a Nigga' mission."

Eric took out a small plastic bag of cocaine, spread it out on a hand mirror on top of the bar counter, and began chopping it up.

LeBaron's eyes bugged. "Yo, what are you doing?" he snapped.

"Minding my own business. Something you should do."

"Eric, don't do it."

"Watch me," he said, snorting a fat line of coke. "Oo, whee!" he yelled. "This is some good shit. You want some?"

"You're an addict," LeBaron said.

"I ain't hooked on coke," Eric joked. "I just like how it smells."

LeBaron walked over and grabbed the mirror.

"You better give me my shit," Eric warned.

LeBaron held it away with one hand as if to dump it. "Or what?"

Eric moved toward him menacingly. "I'm not playing with you. Give me my shit. That's five hundred dollars' worth of coke."

LeBaron backed into the kitchen, holding the mirror aloft. When he got to the sink, Eric jumped on him and tried to wrestle the mirror out of his hand. The mirror fell to the floor and the coke went up in a puff of smoke. Eric tried to punch LeBaron in the face, but LeBaron blocked the jab and spun Eric around and put him in a headlock. Eric pushed off from the counter and slammed LeBaron's back against the wall, knocking down two pictures, the glass shattering. Eric broke free and grabbed a butcher knife from out of the kitchen drawer.

"C'mon, Eric. What are you going to do, stab me?" LeBaron heaved, trying to catch his breath.

"Get the fuck out of here before I do something crazy." Eric had an evil look in his eyes.

LeBaron stared at the butcher knife. "I feel sorry for you, man." He backed out of the kitchen, picked up his bag, and walked to the door. "Eric, people care about you. Don't throw your life away." LeBaron slammed the front door behind him.

The knife fell from Eric's hand. He steadied himself with one hand on the counter. "What is happening to me?" He started to cry. "God help me. I need help."

Eric stared at the pile of coke spread out all over the floor and got down on hands and knees and scooped up as much as he could. He looked at the sink as if to dump it, but instead went over to the bar and began snorting.

LeBaron leaned back into the soft leather seats inside the first-class Amtrak Acela train car. He was on the phone with Phoenix. It was a three-hour ride back to Washington, D.C., plenty of time for him to vent his anger. He was sick of and sorry for Eric.

"Baby, you should have seen him," LeBaron said, sipping a Captain Morgan and Coke. "It was like I was talking to a stranger."

Phoenix was in bed eating a ridiculously big bowl of chocolate ice cream. Bridgitte was lounging in the leather chair across the room, looking at a black hair magazine.

"You *were* talking to a stranger," Phoenix said between gulps. "Drugs turn your friends into fiends."

Bridgitte smiled at the rhyme. Phoenix winked at her.

"You are not going to believe what he did," LeBaron whispered.

Phoenix smirked. "Huh? If it's Eric, I bet I'll believe it."

A white businessman in the aisle across from LeBaron was straining his neck eavesdropping. LeBaron shot him his best "crazy Negro" look and the man jerked back into his seat.

LeBaron put his hand over the phone and lowered his voice. "He snorted some cocaine."

"Eric snorted cocaine right in front of you?" Phoenix screamed, scaring Bridgitte, who dropped the magazine, then also screamed.

"Eric snorted cocaine in front of LeBaron?" Bridgitte jumped onto the bed next to Phoenix.

"Girl, get up off me." Phoenix pushed Bridgitte away.

"Calm down, baby," LeBaron said. "I don't want you to get excited."

"Calm down? He had drugs in there while you were there? What if the cops came and raided the place?"

LeBaron held the phone away from his ear and rolled his eyes. Meanwhile Phoenix continued her rant.

"Then you would have gone right to jail with his ass,

and our baby would have to visit his father in jail. I'm telling you, LeBaron, I'm not visiting your ass in jail."

"Put Bridgitte on the phone for me, please," he said.

"Huh?" Phoenix said.

"Put Bridgitte on the phone."

After a few seconds Bridgitte came on. "What's up, LB?"

"Can you do me a favor before I get home?" he joked.

"Sure, what do you want me to do?" Bridgitte said, sounding confused.

"Can you please slap the shit out of Phoenix for me?"

Chapter Twenty

Eden was nervous as she walked into David Denson's office. She looked at her hands. They were trembling. Her nerves were shot. The stress of her anchoring duties along with worrying about Eric was getting to her.

It's all so clear to me now. How tired he's been looking. His nose bleeding. That slut he had at his apartment. I can't get her skanky voice out of my head. Ugh, I can't stand to even think about him. Lord, I just pray that you bless him with the strength to get off those drugs.

Eden sat down facing David. What did he want? It had been a month since Eden had been subbing for Susan LaFontaine, and she felt as if she had been doing a good job. A lot of great things had happened to her since then. She had been asked to emcee a few charity events and was interviewed for a layout in *Essence* magazine on "Women to Watch" in the media. Her star was definitely on the rise while Eric's was most certainly on the decline.

David got right to the point. "Eden, we want to hire you full-time."

Eden gasped. "Uh, come again?" she stammered.

David smiled. "Your anchoring has been fantastic, and we want you to work for us full-time. Are you interested?"

"Am I interested? Why, yes, I am." She beamed. "But what about Susan?"

He paused to clear his throat. "Don't worry about Susan. She's been wanting some lighter duties for a while."

David stood and shook Eden's hand. "We'll iron out all the details with your agent and Karen. She's going to be mad about us stealing you. But at least you're staying in the ABC family. And right now, your station might not be the best place for you with all that's going on."

Eden was puzzled. "What do you mean?"

It was David's turn to look surprised. "Your coworker. The cokehead. What's his name?" David snapped his fingers trying to recall his name.

"Eric," Eden said softly.

It had been three days since Eric left his apartment. He had been living like a hermit, a grimy hermit. The heavy drapes were shut and sunlight hadn't seen the inside of his place for days. He'd checked his mail only once and that was just to get his copy of *GQ* magazine, one of his favorites. The phone had been off the hook for the last two days. His last conversation with Eden combined with the argument with

LeBaron had left him sullen and depressed. Eric hadn't eaten in two days but wasn't hungry. The steady diet of cocaine and liquor had dulled his appetite. He had a three-day-old growth of beard and his teeth hadn't seen a toothbrush in days.

The living room was as dark as his mood. The only light was from a bathroom down the hall. Eric struggled through red glassy eyes to focus on his wide-screen television. He was watching Eden anchoring the weekend morning news. Eric had TiVo'd her last few shows.

Watching her had been torture. It had been eating him up inside that Eden had rejected him. A woman rejecting Eric Swift? It was something that he couldn't remember ever happening to him. Eric felt his life spiraling out of control. He thought about how ironic it was that his career was now firmly in the bottom of the toilet and Eden's career was headed into the stratosphere.

Maybe it was for the best, because I would have definitely messed up her life.

Eric took a healthy swig from his fifth rum and Coke of the day and tried to stand. His legs wobbled as he made his way to the bathroom to relieve himself. As he walked toward the hallway he noticed an envelope sticking out from under his front door. He bent down but lost his balance and fell headfirst onto the floor. The glass of rum and Coke bounced off the door, splashing the warm liquor all over his face and shirt. Eric managed to pull himself into a sitting position and held the legal-sized envelope in his hand.

"What is this?" he slurred.

It was a letter from the ABC legal department. Eric stared at the envelope like it was laced with anthrax. He reached up and behind him to click on the light switch. He ripped open the letter and in his drunken and high state struggled to read the first line. When it finally registered what he was reading, it knocked him stone cold sober.

Dear Mr. Eric Swift,
This letter is to confirm that your employment with ABC is hereby and immediately terminated.

"Fired?" The word had a terrible taste. "How am I going to tell Pops? Mama is going to be devastated."

Eric flung the letter in the corner and struggled to his feet. He went into the bathroom and splashed cold water on his face. As the water dripped down his face, he stared at his reflection. What he saw hurt his heart. It was the face of defeat.

Chapter Twenty-one

Getting fired is always a terrible thing, but finding out through the mail is humiliating. *Damn, they could have had the balls to at least call a nigga*, Eric thought.

After nearly a week of bingeing on alcohol and coke, Eric figured it was time to take some action. Strangely, he felt like a weight had been lifted off his shoulders. He could start fresh. Maybe he would move out of the city. The dream job in New York had turned into one long nightmare. His first order of business, after cleaning up himself and his apartment, was to check his messages. He had more than a dozen waiting.

"Hi, Eric, this is Carmella. Where have you been, baby?" the sultry voice purred from the answering machine.

In hell.

Eric pressed the next button.

"Hi, Daddy, this is Janet Jackson. Remember me? I'll be in town next weekend and would love to hook up with you. I got a surprise for you. I have a brand-new titanium prosthetic leg. We can't break this one."

Eric rubbed his chin for a moment. "Nah."

He pressed next again.

"Hey, baby, this is Sharon. Call m—"

"Next," Eric said.

"Yo, E? Where the f-f-fuck you been?"

"Spit that shit out, Dirty." Eric laughed, then listened to the next message.

"Eric, this is Spencer. I need to talk to you. It's extremely urgent." It was his agent.

Let me guess, Spencer. I'm fired?

Next.

"Eric, this is your mother. Call me."

Uh-oh. I wonder if she knows that I've been fired. Eric definitely wasn't up for one of her sermons. He went to the next message.

"Eric Lamont Swift," his mother's voice shrieked through the intercom. "Didn't I tell you to call me back?"

Shit, this must be serious. Shirley never called twice. Eric quickly dialed the number. She picked up on the third ring.

"Hello," Shirley said. Her voice was tired.

"Mama, this is Eric."

"I know who this is, boy," she snapped. "I carried you for nine months, I should know your voice."

Oh God, here she goes.

"What's wrong, Mama?"

"You daddy is sick."

"W-what's wrong?" Eric stuttered.

Shirley paused.

"Mama. What's wrong with Dad?"

"Eric, your daddy got cancer."

"Pops got cancer?" He couldn't believe it. The news crushed Eric. It felt like his heart had exploded. His father meant everything to him. Growing up, while other kids worshipped sports or movie stars, Eric idolized David Swift. He was always there for him, never missed a practice or a game. After his mother finished giving him the details of the diagnosis, Eric hung up the phone and slumped down on the sofa in a daze.

A flood of emotions rushed over him. First, the depression of making a fool out of himself and losing Eden, the humiliation of getting fired, the desperation of drugs and alcohol, and now the sobering reality that his father was dying. It was all too much to bear.

God, I can't take any more. If Pops dies, I don't know what I am gon' do. Eric cried like a baby.

As he lay there crying, he thought of the good times they'd shared. David didn't play, he was a man's man and made sure that Eric and his brother would be the same. He ran the house like a drill sergeant. In fact, he was an army infantryman during the Vietnam War. Shirley used to tease Eric about how much he cried when his father was shipped overseas to Germany for his last tour. Since the day David was discharged, father and son had been thick as thieves. He always treated him like an adult. Even when Eric was a young boy his father wouldn't whip him. He had other ways to teach him a lesson. Through tears, Eric laughed as he thought about the time his father busted him with a bag of marijuana.

It was Christmas Day 1987, and Eric's parents were supposed to spend a few days out of town with relatives. He and his brother Sean would have the house to themselves. Eric couldn't wait to get the party started. He had bought a big bag of weed the day before and hid it in his underwear. It was the first time that he'd brought weed into the house. He figured he was good because his parents were supposed to leave at dawn, so he slept with it in his pajamas. But when he woke up Christmas morning he heard the television blaring a western movie, a sure sign that David was still there. When Eric walked into the living room and saw the back of his father's head, he froze.

"Uh, hey, Pop. What you doing here? I thought you and Mom were going out of town."

"I'ma meet her later. I have something to take care of," David said.

Damn, Eric thought. *I have to get this weed out of here.*

He looked out the window and across the street. He saw his best friend, Matthew, cutting the grass. *I'll let Matt hold the weed until Pop leaves*, he thought.

Eric grabbed a robe and ran outside to the fence to pass

off the weed, but when he checked the front of his pajamas he couldn't find the weed.

"Oh shit." He panicked. "I must have dropped it in the bed."

He ran back into the house and flipped the mattress over, threw sheets and pillows all over the room. No weed.

His heart was racing NASCAR style. He casually walked back into the living room, where David was watching television. The back of the chair was facing Eric, and lo and behold right behind the chair was the bag of weed.

Dammit! Eric thought. He had to act quick, because if David got up and saw the weed, he was finished.

"Hey, Pop, what you watching?" he casually asked while kicking the bag of weed into the hallway. David just grunted.

Eric dashed into the hallway, scooped up the weed, and ran to the front door.

"Freeze!" David's booming voice ordered.

Eric froze. "Huh?" He turned with an innocent look on his face. "What's up, Pop?"

"Give it here." David stared knives at him.

Eric acted confused.

"Give it here."

"What are you talking about?"

"Quit fucking around, Eric. Give me the dope," David insisted.

Eric shook his head no. David snatched open Eric's robe and yanked the bag of weed out. Eric was crestfallen.

David exploded and chewed Eric a new asshole, grounding him forever in the process.

"But, Pop, Tonia is coming over and we were going out," Eric pleaded. He and his girlfriend, Tonia, were going to exchange presents and go to the movies later that day.

"I don't give a shit if the president is coming over, your ass is grounded."

Crushed, Eric had to think of a way to explain this to his girlfriend. He couldn't tell her the truth because Tonia didn't know he got high. She thought he was a choirboy. Later that morning when she came over, he lied. Well, sort of.

"Me and Pop got into a big argument and he won't let me use the car," Eric said, opening up the present she had brought for him. It was a gold bracelet with her initials on it.

"Dang, what happened?" she said, frowning.

As Eric started to lie, David walked into the room. "Hey, Mr. Swift." Tonia beamed. She liked Eric's father.

"Merry Christmas, Tonia," David said. He got right to the point. "Guess what I found this morning?" He stared at his son.

I know this nigga ain't about to . . . Eric thought. His knees started knocking.

David held out the bag and let it unroll.

"Oh my God," Tonia gasped. "Mr. Swift, you get high?"

David shook his head no and looked soberly at Eric. Tonia's gaze followed.

Eric gulped. "See, I uh—"

"Eric doesn't get high," Tonia cut him off. "Does he?" she asked Eric's father.

"This was my first time," Eric lied.

David didn't say anything. He didn't have to; Eric's lies were all the incrimination needed. Tonia broke up with him on the spot and ran out of the house.

Remembering the story usually made Eric laugh. This time it made him cry. Wiping the tears from his eyes, he looked at a picture of himself with his father, right after the Redskins drafted him, and said a silent prayer.

Chapter Twenty-two

Eric needed a vacation. He felt the weight of the world upon him while at the same time his own world was falling apart. Eric had dreamed of taking a bite out of the Big Apple and turning it into his very own Garden of Eden. But New York was starting to look like Sodom and Gomorrah, and a change of scenery was in order before he lost his soul. After giving Dirty Dre a key to his apartment with instructions to take care of some minor bills, he set out for his parents' home—for how long, he didn't know. He flirted with the idea of telling LeBaron about his troubles but decided against it. After all, they weren't currently speaking to each other.

Eric's parents lived in Stone Mountain, Georgia, a wealthy black suburb outside Atlanta. He had bought them the nine-room Tudor-style house along with the three manicured acres it sat on with part of his first multi-million-dollar NFL bonus. It felt good to do something for his parents. The mini mansion, located in a gated community, was a far cry from the gritty South Bronx, where he'd spent his early childhood, and the tiny two-bedroom house in Atlanta where he'd lived as a teen.

Eric sat in the rental car parked in front of his parents' house for a few minutes and stared at their front door. He had no idea what he would say to his father or how he would handle seeing him. During the hour and a half plane ride from LaGuardia to ATL, he had come up with a dozen different scenarios, but as Eric pressed the buzzer beside the oak double doors, all of his preconceived thoughts vanished. It took about a minute for the door to slowly creak open.

"Come on in, baby," Shirley said, kissing him on the cheek.

"Hey, Mama." He hugged her.

As Eric dropped his luggage in the foyer, a chill went through him. Although the central air was on, the house seemed stale. It was the stench of sickness.

"How's Daddy?" Shirley smiled. Eric sounded like a little child.

"He's tired, baby, real tired." Her soft brown eyes drifted from her son to a picture hanging on the wall of David during his army days. "The chemo is zapping all of his strength, but yo' daddy is a fighter. God willing, he gon' be alright."

"Where is he?" Eric said nervously.

"In the downstairs guest bedroom."

"The guest bedroom?" Eric shot back.

"Uh-huh. Your daddy's too weak to walk up and down those stairs."

Eric sighed. He felt nauseous. Shirley turned and walked into the kitchen and sat down at the table. She fumbled with a pack of cigarettes.

"Mama, how you doing?" Eric stood behind her, massaging her slender shoulders. "You look tired."

Shirley opened up the half-smoked pack of Lucky Strikes, took one out, lit it up, and took a long drag.

"Son, you don't know the half," she said, blowing weeks of stress as well as smoke in the spacious kitchen. Eric coughed as the smoke raced through his nostrils. He picked up the pack of unfiltered cigarettes, hating that his parents smoked.

"Ma, you need to stop smoking yourself." Eric looked concerned. "One parent with lung cancer is enough."

Shirley sighed. "I know, baby, but going through what I've gone through, I'm lucky I'm not doing drugs."

Eric nervously cleared his throat at that comment.

"But look here, boy," she said, turning around to look up at Eric. "Don't worry 'bout me. Go in there and see your daddy. He's waiting on you."

Eric took a deep breath and headed to the guest bedroom.

"Son?"

"Yeah, Mama?"

"Be strong, son." Shirley cautioned him. "Your daddy doesn't look the same."

As Eric made his way down the hallway to the bedroom, he smiled at the soulful sounds of Bobby Blue Bland pounding through the guest bedroom door.

Pop and his damn blues, he laughed. *His old ass ain't changed a bit.*

Eric's hand shook nervously as he banged on the door. He heard the clank of a glass and a "What the fuck?" come from inside the room. A moment later the music lowered.

"What?" David yelled.

"Pop, it's me. Can I come in?"

"Who in the hell is 'me'?"

Eric smiled and shook his head. "It's Eric, your favorite son."

"Ya mama just told me you ain't my son. I always knew you looked like the milkman," David snapped in jest.

He got cancer and jokes, Eric thought, pushing the door open. Once inside, his heart sank. David looked a lot older than his fifty-six years. A handsome and slender man his entire life, the chemo treatments had caused him to lose a lot of weight and a lot of hair. In fact, David's entire head was shaved.

"What's up, *Michael* Jordan?" Eric joked. He had to, otherwise he'd cry. David struggled to sit up in the bed.

"Nothing much, *Michael* Jackson," he snapped back,

eyeing Eric's multicolored shirt. "You look like you just came back from Neverland Ranch." He coughed. "I hope you ain't bring no kids with you. You remember what happened last time?"

They laughed. Eric felt the tension ease as he realized his father still thought he was Richard Pryor. That much hadn't changed, at least. He always had jokes. Shirley said that's where Eric got his foolishness from.

He walked over to the bed and gently hugged his father, a little too gently for David's taste.

"Damn. Hug me like a man." David pushed off his hands, frowning. "I ain't no baby."

"Sorry, Pop, I was jus—"

"Just my ass." David laughed. Growing up, whenever Eric would make an excuse, he would begin by saying "I was just," and each time his father would cut him off with "just my ass."

"It's good to see you too, Pop." Eric adjusted a pillow behind him.

"Wish it was under better circumstances, son." He wiggled his back into the down-filled pillows.

"It's okay, Pop. We gon' beat this thing."

David raised his eyebrow suspiciously.

"What do you mean 'we'? I'm the one looking like I've been on a hundred-week Jenny Craig plan, not you."

"C'mon, Pop. Quit joking. I'm talking about fighting this thing together. I'm not leaving here until we beat this thing."

David turned up the stereo. "Well, I hope you packed Mike Tyson in your suitcase, 'cause cancer is a mother-fucker. Can't eat, can't sleep, can't . . . you know?" David winked his eye.

Eric threw his hands up. "Hey, hey, hey, too much in-formation."

"Whatever." David laughed. "The sink might be a little old but the plumbing is in good shape."

"You are a dirty old man," Eric teased.

"And you are a dirty young man. See what you have to look forward to?"

Eric ignored the comment and laughed. He loved talk-ing shit with his father. It was a big part of their relation-ship. Eric could see why he was so crazy; he didn't have anything on his old man.

"How long are you going to stay here? What about your job?"

"I took a leave of absence," Eric lied. His father coughed again. Eric ran over to the nightstand and poured him a glass of water. David eyed him hard and took a sip from the cup. If there was one thing that David didn't joke about, it was work. To hear him tell it, he had been work-ing since he was five years old and never took a day off. He'd work full-time at his part-time job while he was on vacation from his full-time job.

"Seriously," Eric pleaded. He felt like he was on trial. "I have eight weeks vacation that I can take."

"Eight weeks?" David nearly coughed up the water.

"Goddamn, what kind of job gives you eight weeks of paid vacation?"

"Don't matter, Pop. Hell, you know I have money. I'm here for you."

"But damn, son, you need to keep working."

Eric sat at the foot of the bed and kicked his shoes off.

"Tell me one good reason why I need to keep working." He took the glass of water from his father.

"To pay my damn bills," David joked.

Eric tiptoed toward the bedroom door. He didn't want to wake his father. He needed to rest. They had laughed and talked all afternoon until David fell asleep. As he gently closed the door, Eric could hear David's labored breathing. It took everything in his power not to break down crying. Eric sighed and walked upstairs to his room. Shirley always kept it prepared for him. Locking the door behind him, Eric unpacked. He then went into the spacious bathroom and turned on the shower. The bathroom was the size of a large studio apartment, complete with lounge chairs, a Jacuzzi, a stand-alone shower with front and back jets, plus a twenty-inch plasma television built into the wall.

Eric pulled a small pack of cocaine from his travel bag. After spreading the thin white lines on a hand mirror, he turned on the faucet in the Jacuzzi. He undressed down to a pair of silk Jockey boxers and sat down on a nearby chair. Leaning his head back against the marble wall, he closed his eyes. A million thoughts ran through his mind. He thought he heard voices.

What are you doing disrespecting your mama's house?

Your life's a fucking joke and a lie.

You really need to leave that coke alone.

"I can't. That shit be calling me," Eric said to himself. Then he heard his father's voice.

Son, I need you.

He stood up and in a wide sweeping motion knocked the coke into the sink and hurriedly turned on the faucet. Eric cupped the stream of water in his hands and splashed his face. Warm tears mixed with the cool water.

Chapter Twenty-three

The next morning Eric was up bright and early. Actually, he never really went to sleep. He tossed and turned all night thinking about David. Eric was nervous about taking his father to his chemotherapy treatment that morning. He hoped that he could handle seeing his father undergo the energy-sapping process. Eric couldn't get the thin, frail image of his father out of his mind. David had always been a source and a symbol of strength to him. He looked up to his father as if he was a superhero and prayed that cancer wouldn't turn out to be his kryptonite.

Eric helped his father into the SUV. David loved trucks and Eric made sure he had a new one every two years. David was particularly enamored of his six-month-old white Cadillac Escalade. "Makes me feel like I own the road," he'd always say. David hadn't been doing much driving lately.

The trip was going to be more than an hour and a half ride to the doctor's office in Marietta, and Eric knew traffic would move at a snail's pace. Eric flipped through the CD case he'd packed.

"Whatcha' doing?" David asked. He looked at Eric like he was a shoplifter.

"What do you mean?" Eric said, confused. "I'm getting a CD out."

"Whatcha' got?" David was skeptical.

"Hmm, let's see." Eric flipped a few more, then paused. "Got some Wu Tang."

"Some Wu who?"

Okay . . . no Wu Tang for Pops, Eric thought. "Okay, Pop, what about some Jay-Z?"

David yanked the CD case away from Eric and threw it in the backseat. "Jay-Z, you must be Cray-Z. You ain't playing none of that hippity-hoppity shit in my truck. I already have to go to chemo. You want me to have to wear a damn Miracle Ear too?" He laughed.

David pressed the play button on the truck's stereo and Clarence Carter's blues classic, "I Be Strokin'," came blasting out.

Eric quickly covered his ears. "Whoa, is that garbage?" he yelled.

David looked at his son like he was an alien. "That, my boy, is old school." He then sang out loud to the song.

Eric shook his head and turned the ignition. "Nah, old man. That ain't old school; that music is prehistoric."

David ignored him and kept singing. His off-key harmony was killing Eric's ears.

"Hey, Pop?" he interrupted. "What do you sing, alto, bass?"

"Huh?" David said, turning down the volume.

"What do you sing, alto or bass?"

"I don't know," he said, annoyed.

"You should sing tenor," Eric said.

"Why?"

"Ten or . . . eleven miles away, so I don't have to hear that shit." Eric cracked up laughing.

"Ya think you're funny, huh?" David smirked.

"I'd have to say that I'm very funny." Eric cheesed while admiring his reflection in the rearview mirror.

"Yeah, you've always been funny," David mumbled while turning the volume back up. "Funny looking."

"Huh? What did you say?" Eric asked, leaning over.

"Nothing," David said, twisting the volume knob louder. "I just said kiss my black ass."

Eric nodded, keeping his eyes on the road. After a half hour of listening to the best of the blues, David suddenly turned off the radio. It was as if an idea popped into his mind. He stared at his son.

"Whatcha' looking at me like that for, Pop?" Eric asked nervously.

"I was just wondering something, son. You haven't said anything 'bout your job."

Eric felt his face flush. "Um, what do you mean? It's

okay. I mean, it's a job," he managed to stumble. *I wonder if Pop knows*, he thought nervously. *It would be just like him to fuck with my head.*

David wouldn't let up. "You always talked about your job in D.C. When you got that big job in New York, your ass wouldn't shut up about it." He was eyeing Eric real hard.

"Damn, Pop, why you sweating me? The job is alright, a whole lot more stressful than in D.C., that's for sho'."

"How so?"

"Damn, am I on trial?"

"Should you be?" David shot back.

Damn, this nigga think he Matlock, Eric thought. "Pop, it's all good," he said, keeping an eye on the road. "I'm making a shitload of money and I'm on TV every day. What else is there to say?"

David pulled a pillow from out of a gym bag and placed it between his head and the window. His medication was making him groggy. "If you say so, son, but you can't bull-shit a bullshitter," he said before nodding off. Every mile or so Eric looked over at his snoozing father.

If Pop finds out I got fired, or, worse yet, why I got fired, it's gon' sho' nuff kill him.

Eric made it to the doctor's office just in time for the appointment. The medical center was plush and family friendly. Large windows allowed the bright sunlight to fill the waiting area. The soft, soothing jazz was a nice touch too. After helping his father get settled in the patient area, he tracked down Dr. John Stevens, David's oncologist. If Hollywood was casting for a doctor, it could do no better than Dr. Stevens. He could have played a handsome doctor on the hit drama series *ER*. Dr. Stevens was tall, at least six two, lean, and had a full head of salt and pepper hair. During the sleepless night before, Eric had searched for hours on the Internet reading everything he could find about him. Dr. Stevens was a first-rate surgeon and one of the leading cancer doctors in the nation. Knowing that, Eric still grilled him about David's prognosis and myriad treatment options he'd downloaded. Dr. Stevens was cautiously optimistic and told Eric that David had a very good chance of beating the lung cancer. His team had detected it early and the chemotherapy seemed to be making progress. Looking at how sick and weak his father was, Eric couldn't help but wonder how he would look if the chemo wasn't working. He waved to his father as the nurses wheeled David to the treatment room. It was such a nice day, Eric chose to wait outside in the truck. Besides, he couldn't bear to see his father go through the treatment.

Since he had a couple of hours to kill, he pulled out a journal from his bag. He'd picked up the leather-bound journal along with an expensive Waterman ink pen in the airport. He had read in a *GQ* article on stress that when dealing with an emotional crisis it was therapeutic to write down your thoughts, then study them. There was a questionnaire along with the article. He ripped it and the article out and kept them. Since he had found out about his father, Eric had resolved to get his life together. Even he knew that he was heading down a dark path. His life had been blessed, and he felt he needed to be more in touch with his spirituality. It was something he had rarely thought about doing. Anybody who knew Eric would think that the only things he got in touch with were women and shot glasses. He leaned the comfortable leather seat back, stretched his lanky six three frame, and stared at the empty pad. His attention wandered to the sight of people walking in and out of the medical center's front door, their expressions ranging from grim to ecstatic. Eric thought about how thin the line between the two was.

"Maybe I should go see a therapist like LeBaron did." He laughed. "Hell no!" He continued staring at the pad. The blank page seemed to be mocking him, daring him to write. Eric was getting frustrated.

"I can't do this." He flung the journal into the passenger seat. "Where do I start? Where do I start?" he said out loud while banging his fists on the steering wheel. An elderly couple walking by the truck stared at Eric like he was crazy. He didn't even notice them. Eric dug into the bag and fished out the *GQ* article and questionnaire. He carefully unfolded it and read it. He focused on a passage that said to be honest and write down the one thing that you don't want anyone to know about you. Eric stroked his chin for a moment, then wrote down *I masturbate daily.*

After letting out a hearty laugh, he ripped the page out of the journal and balled it up. He scribbled a short heading, *Eric's Journal Entry #1.*

Let's see . . . what's the one thing that I don't want anybody to know about my situation? I don't want anybody to know that I got fired.

Eric kept reading. The rest of the passage instructed the person to answer the question *Why not?* He continued writing. *Because it would be embarrassing.*

Eric glanced back at the article. It said to then answer the question *Why?*

"Hell, that's easy." He chuckled as he wrote: *It would be embarrassing because I have a fly-ass image to protect.*

He looked at the article again. The next passage read *Is hiding that secret worth suppressing your happiness and well-being?*

Eric stared in disbelief at the article.

"What is this? Some trick shit!" he said. But after thinking about it for a few seconds, Eric smiled. It felt kind of freeing to be writing his intimate feelings down. He thought about other things that he didn't want people to know about him. Eric scribbled down, *I don't want people to know that I use drugs.* He paused, then continued, *Because they will think that I am a messed-up person.* Eric stopped. "I need to be more honest," he mumbled. He then wrote a very personal passage that began with a phrase very few men would ever admit: *I am a sorry excuse for a man.* He then scribbled, *I wonder what Eden's doing?* in the margin.

Chapter Twenty-four

"Just move a little to the left . . . smile. Yeah, that's it," the photographer from *Elle* magazine purred. "Eden, sweetheart, you look faaaaabulous."

Eden laughed at the way he said *fabulous*. She felt fabulous too. She was being photographed while sitting behind the anchor desk, decked out in a canary yellow Chanel pantsuit with matching silk shirt. Eden was a natural model and easily glided through the photo session. She was being profiled as part of an article on women making headlines in their professions. She thought about Eric, who was making headlines of his own. *I wonder how he's doing. Lord, I ask you again to bless him and to bless me with a man who's just like him but who isn't on drugs.*

"Eden?" The photographer snapped his fingers. "C'mon, girl, quit daydreaming."

"Sorry." She smiled.

This was Eden's third layout in the last month. First it was *Essence*, then *Ebony*, now she was gracing the pages of white magazines. She was a long way from her first job as a low-paid reporter chasing fires and water main breaks.

Eden loved the network. It agreed with her. It took her all of two days to get used to the limo service, personal assistant, and hairstylist. She had expected those things, but the one thing she had no idea about was how much money she was going to get paid. She had almost choked when her agent showed her the contract. Eden was going to get paid $950,000 a year.

Chapter Twenty-five

Eric had a wide smile as he smelled the sweet aroma of his mother's cooking. The spicy scent of crawfish étouffée, Eric's favorite dish, wafted through the kitchen.

"Mama, you really put your foot in the pot," Eric said, rubbing his stomach.

"Thank you, baby," she said, tasting the spoon.

As Eric sat down at the table, a worried look crossed his face. He had spent half the day at the medical center with his father. The whole ordeal left him drained. Seeing his dejected look, Shirley took off her apron and sat down across from him.

"What's wrong, baby. Is it your daddy?"

He nodded his head yes.

"Son, it's in the hands of the good Lord."

"I know, Mama." Eric sighed. "But I can't get over how bad Daddy looks. You should have seen him on the way home. He was so out of it, I couldn't understand a word he said."

"Hrumph!" she snorted. "I've seen it, alright. It's the same when I take him. Lamont, baby, I'm at the end of my rope. It's killing me to see him like this. Sometimes he's so sick he can't even get up out of the bed and go to the bathroom."

Eric shook his head in pity. They both looked up, hearing the shuffling sounds of slippers scraping the hallway, accompanied by an elderly voice humming a church hymn.

"Is that—?" Eric asked.

Shirley nodded yes. Eric rolled his eyes.

It was the footsteps of Mo' Jessie, Eric's grandmother and Shirley's mother. Eric always had a strange relationship with her. Sometimes she could be a little too blunt for his liking. Jessica Lee Landry was up visiting from New Orleans and was coming from the back room where David was sleeping.

"Well," Mo' Jessie said, opening the refrigerator and pulling out a pitcher of purple Kool-Aid. "Looks like David is gon' die, so I guess the next time I'll be back will be for the funeral. By the way, what time does *Oprah* come on here?" She nonchalantly poured a tall glass as Eric and Shirley sat stunned.

"What?" Mo' Jessie asked, looking at them.

Shirley's eyes were bugging. Eric was furious. He stormed out of the room. Mo' Jessie shrugged her shoulders as if to say "What did I say wrong?"

Eric shouldn't have been surprised. Mo' Jessie always said exactly what was on her mind, and damn what anybody else thought about it. She had had a hard life growing up in the backwoods bayou and had no time for niceties. Mo' Jessie was fond of saying, "I've picked cotton for ten cents a day. Buried two ex-husbands and two sons. I ain't got time to cry."

"Mama, I can't believe you said that in front of that boy," Shirley snapped. "You know how he is about his daddy."

Mo' Jessie was nonplussed. "Look, ya'll better just prepare for the worst, that's all."

"But you didn't have to say it like that."

"Look, I'm sixty-five years old. I'll say whatever I damn well please."

There was no use arguing with Mo' Jessie. Shirley got up and went back to the stove. Mo' Jessie gulped the last of her Kool-Aid and shuffled back to her room, mumbling something about *Oprah*.

Chapter Twenty-six

It had been weeks since Eric had used any drugs, but not a day had gone by without him thinking about cocaine. And lately, the cravings were getting stronger. There were two things preventing him from giving in to temptation. One was that Eric didn't want to disrespect his parents' house by doing drugs there. Besides, he knew he couldn't disguise being high. His father always saw right through him. The next and main reason was that he didn't have access to any drugs. Eric didn't know any drug dealers in the Atlanta area and definitely wasn't going to buy it off the street and risk getting arrested. Still, his urges were such that he decided to seek professional help. As he sat on his bed, he thumbed through the yellow pages, searching for Narcotics Anonymous.

"Damn, how many drug treatment places are there?" There were hundreds of listings for addiction help. The choices ranged from expensive rehab centers to free clinics.

I'm not checking myself into rehab. I want a free anonymous phone conversation. He flipped through a few more pages. *Narcotics Anonymous, there it is.*

Eric reached for the phone. "No, I can't use my mama's phone," he mumbled. "They might have caller ID and call back."

He grabbed his cell phone, but before he dialed the number he cracked open the bedroom door and peered out. His mother and father were in their room down the hall and there was no sign of Mo' Jessie. Eric quietly closed the door and locked it. To make sure that no one could easily overhear his conversation, he turned on the stereo. Eric was nervous as he dialed the 800 number.

"No," he said, pressing end. "I can't do this." He tossed the phone on the bed and fell back. The soft mattress was comfortable. Eric stared at the ceiling.

I'm not an addict. I don't need any help. What I need is some coke. He sighed. *Damn, there has to be somebody around here I can score from. I just need a few lines. Nothing major and I'll be alright.*

"No." He jerked upright, reaching for his cell phone. "I need some help."

He pressed redial. His call was answered on the first ring. "Narcotics Anonymous," the male voice answered.

Eric was silent.

"Hello?" the male voice asked. He heard Eric breathing. "It's okay, I'm here to help."

"I'm, uh . . ." Eric struggled.

"You're in need of help?" the male voice said.

"Yes," Eric said. "I need some help."

"Sir, my name is Robert. You don't have to tell me your name. Right now that's not important. What's important is that you've taken the first step to cure yourself. Can I ask you a question?"

"Yes."

"What drugs are you using?"

"Cocaine," Eric admitted. It felt weird yet liberating to be admitting his problem to a total stranger.

"Let me tell you about who we are. We're a nonprofit fellowship for whom drugs has become a major problem. We are recovering addicts who meet regularly to help each other stay clean. There is only one requirement for membership, the desire to stop using."

"But I don't think that I am an addict," Eric said.

"Of course you don't. That's what all addicts think. An addict is a man or woman whose life is controlled by drugs."

"But my life isn't controlled by drugs."

"Why did you call?" Robert asked.

"Because I need help." Eric frowned.

"Help for what?"

"To get off drugs. What do you think?"

Robert's voice was calm and controlled. "Why do you want to get off drugs?"

"Because I can't stop thinking about cocaine."

"So cocaine is controlling you?"

"Yes!" As soon as he said it, Eric shook his head in disgust. "I guess I am an addict."

"There's nothing to be ashamed about. We all have to admit it eventually."

Eric cut him off. "But I'm not all strung out or stealing from my family to support my habit."

"Drugs affect individuals differently. Some people become hooked immediately and their life spirals out of control. For others, it takes longer. One thing is certain. Eventually, drugs will defeat you. You will lose your job, you will hurt the ones you love."

Eric nodded. He knew exactly what Robert was talking about. Robert proceeded to tell Eric about his own battle with heroin. The story of how he lost his wife and kids touched Eric at his core. Robert also didn't prod Eric too much but allowed him to reveal his situation in his own time. Eric was honest without giving up any information about his real identity. Robert invited him to a meeting. Eric scribbled the information on the back of an envelope. After hanging up, he stared at it.

"I'm not going to any damn meetings," he said before balling up the paper in his hand.

For most of the afternoon, Eric stayed in his room thinking and researching what Robert had said. He went online to the Narcotics Anonymous website. One thing that stood out were the twelve principles on which the group was founded. The first principle stated, "We admitted that we were powerless over our addiction, that our lives had become unmanageable." Eric could relate to that because his life was out of control. The second principle read, "We made a decision to turn our will and our lives over to the care of God." And another one was to make a list of the people he had hurt and become willing to make amends to them all. One name came immediately to mind. Eden.

One day I am going to apologize to her.

He logged off and cursed himself for missing out on a good woman. He vowed not to let another good woman slip through his fingers. As he paced the room, an old family photo album caught his eye. Eric opened it and spent a half hour flipping through memory lane. It got his mind off Eden and cocaine.

"Oh shit, I remember this picture." Eric laughed at the old snapshot of him and Sean as little boys in front of the Christmas tree. Judging by the thickness of the old worn and frayed leather album, Shirley must have kept every photo they had ever taken. Eric shook his head at the anorexic tree. *A skinny-ass silver Christmas tree. That's some ghetto shit.*

One particular picture made him pause. It was a senior prom picture of him and his first real true love. Her name was Melissa.

A nostalgic smile crossed his face. *I wonder what she's doing these days.*

It had been years since he had even thought of Melissa.

If one woman had ever made him want to get married, it was Melissa. He had always thought of her as the perfect woman. Blessed with exotic features and a body like the pyramids, she was built for the ages. Her mother was Hawaiian and her father was all Negro. Shirley loved Melissa. They even used to go to church together. Eric's mind began to drift.

It was the summer of 1988 when he met Melissa on a hot Sunday night at the roller-skating rink. It was after 9 PM and the rink had just turned into a dance floor. She looked so beautiful, standing there all by herself like the last box of Fruity Pebbles on a grocery store shelf. Eric's favorite cereal.

When he first saw her, Eric was with his best friend, Donovan. "Who is that?" he asked hungrily.

"I don't know," Donovan cracked. "But if I had to guess, a girl who looks like she wouldn't want yo' broke ass."

"Whatever," Eric said, walking straight in her direction. When he reached her he leaned over and whispered, "If I told you that you had a beautiful body, would you hold it against me?"

She just stared at him.

"Wasn't cute, huh?" he said.

"Not even close," she said dismissively.

"Black women sure do know how to make a brother feel stupid. That's why brothers be dating white girls."

"And I care?" Melissa said. Cheryl Lynn's "Got to Be Real" was playing in the background.

190

"Would you like to dance?"

She smacked her bubblegum. "Nope."

"C'mon, don't diss me. All my boys are looking over here, puh-leeze? If you don't I'ma start doing the Wop right here in front of you." Eric started moving his shoulders left to right.

That made her smile. "C'mon, crazy-ass boy."

Eric was king of a dance called "The Prep" and he prepped Melissa's ass all over the dance floor. They danced for two songs and then Luther Vandross's hit "If Only for One Night" came on.

Thank you, God.

Melissa started walking away, but he grabbed her hand. "C'mon, one dance?" he pleaded.

She shook her head no. "I don't slow dance with strangers."

He straightened up. "In that case, allow me to introduce myself. My name is Eric Swift, and don't worry, I'm a Christian."

She laughed and slid into his arms. She smelled all grown-up, just like somebody's mama's perfume.

While "If Only for One Night" was playing, Eric was thinking, *If only for about eight minutes.*

"Do you have a boyfriend?" he whispered.

"Yes."

Damn!

"Why does he let a fine-ass woman like you come out here all by yourself?"

"He didn't—he's here."

Shit!

Eric cleared his throat and glanced around nervously over her shoulder.

"Oh, really? Then why aren't you dancing with him?"

"He can't come inside the skating rink. They banned him."

Fuck!

Eric was scared now. "W-w-why?" he stuttered.

" 'Cause he always be fighting and stuff," Melissa said, while nonchalantly chewing her bubblegum. It's funny how when women describe their crazy-ass boyfriends, it's always in that calm, nonchalant voice.

"Who is your boyfriend?"

"They call him Boogie," she said. "But the warden at the county jail calls him Inmate #37489."

Damn, shit, fuck . . . I'm a dead man.

Eric was slow dancing with the girlfriend of one of the craziest guys at his high school. Boogie fought like regular people breathed. It came naturally to him, like a talent for playing the sax or pitching a ball, and he had no choice but to do it. As soon as the song was over, Eric said, "Goodbye, good luck, have a nice life, and I hope he doesn't kill you."

He saw Melissa out every now and then. They would casually speak for a minute and go on their way, until one night at a Maze and Frankie Beverly concert.

"Hey, Eric," Melissa called out to him.

After scanning the vicinity for the potential "Boogie Beatdown," Eric walked over. That's when Melissa whispered the three magic words he dreamed of hearing her say in his ear: "Boogie's in jail."

After that they were inseparable. Eric sighed as he looked at their graduation picture. *Boy, did I screw that up.*

He did. Eric had promised Melissa that they'd be together forever. They lasted until he got drafted by the NFL. With too much money and too much stardom at a much too young age, Eric strayed. More like he was blown off course. Melissa wasn't one to take his cheating, so she dumped him. It floored Eric. He begged forgiveness. Melissa gave in, but once again Eric cheated, this time with her cousin. And Melissa left him for good. It floored him. After that he vowed to never settle down with one woman again.

A thought popped into Eric's head. He would start dating Melissa. She would get Eric's mind off Eden.

"I'ma call her. I bet her mama will give me her number."

Eric found Melissa's mother's old number in his big black book. Actually, it was a three-ring binder. He dialed the number excitedly. Agnes, Melissa's mother, picked up on the third ring.

"God bless, hello," she said.

Eric smiled. *I see she's still religious.* "Ms. Ford, my name is Eric Swift. You may not remem—"

"Sweet mother of Jesus," she half screamed, cutting

him off. "I remember you, Eric. How ya mama and nem?"

Melissa's mother loved Eric still. Maybe it was because he was the only boyfriend Melissa had ever had who didn't live where you had to pass through a metal detector to visit.

"They fine." He grinned.

"Boy, where you at? Are you in town?"

"Yes, ma'am."

"Melissa's gon' be so happy to talk to you."

"Does she still live here?"

"Yes, baby, she's here." She yelled upstairs for Melissa to come down.

Yes! he thought. *I won't mess it up this time.*

Eric could hear the old stairs creaking as Melissa came down.

"A handsome caller on the line," her mother said, handing her the phone.

"Hello, Boo Bear," Eric said, using his pet name for her.

"Eric!" Melissa screamed. "Boy, what you doing calling me?"

"I miss you," he said.

Melissa was excited. "I miss you too."

I still got it! He began thinking about the buck-wild sex they were sure to have later that night.

"Boo Bear, how are you?" he asked.

"Pregnant."

"Huh?" Eric gasped. He sounded like the wind had been knocked out of him.

"I'm pregnant."

"How many months?" he asked, holding out hope.

"Seven months."

"Uh, dang." He groped for words. "That's, uh, good . . . great."

Melissa remained silent.

"Um . . . who's the father?" Eric asked.

Melissa cleared her throat. "Boogie."

The news hit Eric like a left hook to the jaw. *Can I get just one lucky break while I'm home?*

Chapter Twenty-seven

Eric woke up early the next morning. He had gone to bed early, one of only a few times he had ever done that. But it hadn't been a restful sleep.

"What's wrong, baby?" Shirley had asked, softly knocking at his door.

"Nothing, Mama, just a little tired," Eric said.

"You want some soup?"

"No thanks."

It felt good to be home, but Eric hated that cancer was the reason. He and David were spending a lot of time together. He was very grateful for the time they were sharing. He and his father had always been close, but mortality has a way of taking even familial relationships to new heights. One of the things Eric looked forward to the most was their morning walk through the neighborhood park. Lasting a little more than an hour, the walk allowed them time to talk about a variety of things, like sports, politics, and life.

"Pops? Have you ever felt like you've lost your swagger?" Eric asked, kicking a large pinecone out of his path. It was a cool weekday morning, and they were walking on the park's nature trail. The scene was right out of a Norman Rockwell painting, as autumn had begun to transform the green leaves into golden browns and burnt oranges. David pondered the question for a few seconds before smiling. "Son, you'll lose and find your swagger dozens of times by the time you get to my age. What's the problem this time?"

"Women." Eric sighed. "What else?"

David stroked the gray hairs on his chin. "Ah, man's eternal dilemma. But I've never known you to let women get to you."

Eric nodded in agreement. "Tell me about it. I've been striking out a lot lately, and it's starting to affect everything in my life."

"It should."

"Huh? What is that supposed to mean, Pops?"

"Son, you're getting too old to be chasing after all these women. You should have gotten that out of your system by now. That's cute while you're in your teens and early twenties, but by the time you hit thirty, you should be living your life's purpose."

"I hear you, Pops, but what if I don't know what my purpose is?"

"Then you should pray about it."

Eric threw up his hands in resignation. "That's all I'm hearing lately. Pray about this, pray about that. I have been praying and ain't nothing happening."

"It's not going to happen in your time. Prayers are answered on God's time."

"When did you become Aristotle?"

David coughed and zipped his fleece sweater up to his neck. "Cancer will make a philosopher out of any man. Let me share a story with you, son. When I first found out that I had cancer, I was filled with self-pity. I don't want to die. I didn't know what to do or where to turn. Now, you know I've never really been into the church, but I've always had a personal relationship with God."

"Of course."

"I used to read everything but the Bible. I've questioned everything but the reason why I question everything."

Eric nudged his arm. "What about the damn dinosaurs?" He was alluding to their joke about why the big reptiles aren't mentioned in the Bible.

"Dinosaurs, right." David laughed. "I'm the type of man who needs answers. But let me tell you one thing. The prospect of death has a way of answering every one of my questions."

Eric had a perplexed look on his face. "I'm not following you, Pops."

David motioned for them to sit down. He eased himself

onto a nearby park bench. "Son, when you're facing death, the only thing you're thinking about is God. Questions like Why am I here? What's my purpose in life? It comes back to God. Have I done all that I could have with my life? Have I used the talents that God gave me to the best of my abilities? You realize that time is fleeting, that time is running out. Everything is so clear, and so instead of succumbing to the self-pity, I now understand that the cancer is allowing me to tie up the loose ends of my life. Sort of like a grace period, no pun intended. Ask yourself, Eric, what you have been pursuing throughout your life."

His son was silent as he searched for an answer. "Honestly, I have to say wealth, pleasure."

"Women?" his father added.

"Right, women."

"There," David said. "When you pursue earthly things, you will encounter earthly problems. Eric, you have so many talents, but you've been using them to pursue trivial things. I think these problems are your grace period."

"How long does the grace period last?"

"Only God knows." David stood to stretch. "But one thing is certain."

"What's that, Pops?"

"When the time runs out, you'll be the first one to know."

Chapter Twenty-eight

Eric's Journal

It's been nearly three months since I've been home and I feel confident that I will get my shit together. Hell, it can't get any worse. But it is nice to get away from New York and all its distractions (women, drugs, booze), although there are some fine-ass women in Atlanta. It's taken a lot of willpower and prayer not to go to Magic City. But chasing ass is not my focus. That's what got me into this mess in the first place. This is very hard for me to admit, but I don't care if I meet any women while I'm here because my priorities are to be there for Pop, then to get myself together mentally, physically, and spiritually.

In my opinion, it's been real touch and go for Pop, but he seems to be making some progress. He's not as tired or cranky, and he says he's not in that much pain, but he may just be saying that to keep us from worrying so much. Mama is holding up fine. She's a rock. I really admire her because being around somebody with cancer is a muthafucka. To be able to put up with that has to be hard as hell. Hell, I wanted to knock Pop's ass out once or twice. Hopefully I'll be lucky enough to have a strong woman like her someday.

The best part about being here is that I haven't snorted any cocaine, although if I knew where to get some I might test a little bit to see if it still smells the same. I'm just kidding, I think. I hope. I pray. I can't believe how hard it is to stay away from that shit. I don't care what anybody says. Cocaine may be bad for you, but cocaine is some good shit. Makes a nigga feel superhuman, and the best part is you can have sex all night! I can't believe that I was damn near hooked on that shit. But I'm lucky. That shit could kill a nigga. I'm glad that was all I tried. I damn sure wasn't about to smoke some crack or some bullshit like that. Hey, what did Whitney say? Crack is wack! Hell, I'm too fly to be on some Pookie from New Jack City shit.

At some point, I am going to have to admit to my parents the real reason I've been off work for so long. I don't think Mama has a clue, but Pop doesn't believe I'm on a break for shit. He always knew when I was lying, but he's just too weak to press it. I better leave before his slick ass gets too strong and he hypnotizes my ass into telling the truth.

Let me just add this to my journal. My grandmother Mo' Jessie is outta fucking control! I love her to death, she's damn near like a mother to me, but I'm glad her ass went back home to New Orleans. She was on some real "let's prepare a funeral" shit. Talking about what type of caskets we should get and all this "voodoo" shit. She told me that if I wanted to give somebody bad *luck, that I should take a pair of their drawers and bury it in a graveyard. What kind of Michael Jackson "Thriller" shit is that? I tell you one thing, though. I'ma steal one of Eden's thongs when I get back to New York. Nah, I'm just playing. I think her rejecting me is one of the best things to happen to me. She really turned the tables on a nigga. I was real fucked up for a minute. She had a nigga feeling Babyface. I'm still pissed that I didn't get to have sex with her, but maybe that's for the better. She was way too nice for me. I would have ruined her. I do owe her for taking me to church and getting me to think about God and my spirituality. I really needed that. I'm getting too old to be playing around. I think that God has a higher purpose for me. I'm just not sure what it is. Maybe God wants me to be a preacher. Now, wouldn't that be something? The Reverend Eric Swift.*

Seriously, I have been reading the Bible more, and when I get back to New York I want to look up that Reverend Francois and go to his church. He had the kind of message that I can relate to. Can you imagine Eric the player going to church? God truly works in mysterious ways, or maybe the world is definitely about to end.

Chapter Twenty-nine

As the months passed by father and son became inseparable. Eric, in effect, became his father's chauffeur, driving him to and from treatments and running his errands. He also became his confidant. David's illness was forging a bond that made them tighter than ever.

Today's walk in the park felt extra special. Admiring the view along the tree-lined man-made lake as they strolled, David suddenly felt a new burst of energy. Instead of stopping to rest at the one-mile mark as usual, he pushed the pace. Even though he walked with the aid of a cane, David wanted to power walk the entire two and a half miles around the lake. Eric struggled to keep up with his old man. He was tired and tried to play it off but David was feeling his oats and getting stronger by the step. He had recently been gaining weight and his rapierlike wit was sharper than ever.

"What's wrong," David teased his son. "Are you out of breath?"

"Whatever. I'll walk your old ass in the ground." Eric heaved while bending over to rest both hands on his knees. "But first I'ma take me a lil' break."

"Pussy," David yelled over his shoulder.

Eric ignored the comment as he limped over to a bench to stretch out. He wiped sweat from his eyes. The temperature was near ninety degrees and the noon sun was beaming. As Eric watched his father circle the lake, he reflected on how close he had come to losing him. He was thankful. He said a silent prayer.

Thank you, God. I don't know what I would have done if he had died.

He marveled at his father's newfound vigor. Eric was tired and listless all the time. It was as if he was the one undergoing chemotherapy. He wondered if he was going through some type of drug or alcohol withdrawal. He vowed to try a little of that Ensure that his father swigged all day. After about thirty minutes David plopped down next to his son.

"Move." David nudged his son to scoot over. "I'm tired as a slave at sundown." He pulled a handkerchief out and wiped the sweat from his forehead. "It's so hot I just saw the devil buck naked in the back of an ice-cream truck." He snatched a bottled water from out of Eric's hands.

"Watch it, old dude." Eric smiled.

David stared at his son.

"What?" Eric cracked.

"When were you going to tell me that they fired your ass?"

"Huh?" Eric coughed.

"Huh my ass. I didn't stutter."

"Who told you that?" Eric was getting defensive.

"I'm asking the questions," David snapped.

"Aw shit, Pop . . . I didn't want to tell you."

David continued to stare at him. Eric felt as if he was being cross-examined.

"Okay . . . okay . . . they fired me. There! Are you happy?"

"Don't get mad at me. I'm not the one who fired your ass. But I feel like firing your ass as my son."

Eric rolled his eyes.

"What? Are you rolling your beady-ass eyes at me?" David uneasily stood and held up his cane. "You don't think I won't . . . Boy, you ain't too grown for an ass whipping."

Eric reached out for his arm. "C'mon, Pop. Quit tripping."

"Get your hands off me. I'm real disappointed in you, son."

"Shit, I'm disappointed in myself," Eric said. His eyes were focused squarely on the ground.

"Son, the papers say you're on drugs. Is that true?"

"Pop, how long have you known?" Eric paused. He quickly debated the pros and cons of lying and decided to come clean. "Yes, it's true. But, Pops, I ain't no crack—"

"But Pops my ass," David cut him off. "You threw away a good-ass job like that for some damn drugs? Boy, you've done some dumb shit in your life, but this ranks up there as the dumbest."

"You're absolutely right."

"Goddamn right I'm right." David ranted. "You got any money left or did you smoke it all up?"

Eric winced. "I wasn't smoking crack."

"What was you doing? Her-ron? I bet your ass was smoking that dust. Had to be to do some dumb shit like that."

"It was coke."

"Cocaine! You was snorting cocaine? I bet you was fucking a white woman too, huh? How many times have I told you that there are two things a black man can't handle—white women and cocaine."

"Pop, c'mon."

"Shut up, with your dumb ass . . . blowing all of your money on drugs and bitches."

"Whatever. It doesn't matter. I'm still rich and I'm clean. I haven't done drugs since I've been here."

"Probably 'cause your ass can't find any. I better check my medicine. Your crackhead ass probably done took some of my shit."

"Pops, I'm clean."

"Clean?" David was skeptical.

"I know this is going to sound crazy, but this was the best thing to happen to me."

"Eric, I know that I only finished the third grade, so excuse me if I don't understand how getting your ass busted for drugs and losing your goddamn job was the best thing that ever happened to you."

Eric paused and rubbed his chin. Then he blurted out, "Pops, God is talking to me."

David turned to face Eric. "How so, son?"

"I know that God is bringing this on me so that I can get my life together. But, Pops, sometimes I think that I am a lost cause."

"Son, we all feel that way sometimes."

"But I look at you and see what I could become. I'm just not as strong as you are."

"I'm not Superman. I've had my share of struggles."

"Of course, but I'm not talking about racism and growing up poor. That's different than what I'm talking about."

David smacked Eric upside his head.

"Ouch! What you do that for?"

David shook his head. "Sometimes, I really do wonder if you're my son. Boy, let me tell you a story. When I was a young man I was a hell-raiser."

"I know, Pop. Everybody knows that."

"Do you know that I was locked up?"

Eric's eyes went wide. "What?"

"Yep. I did a year in jail. This was before you were born."

Eric was stunned. "For what?"

"I stabbed a man in a bar fight."

"Killed him?"

"Damn near," David said. "I was drunk as hell, and he tried to cheat me out of some money in a game of pool."

"Who was it?"

"Doesn't matter. What matters is that by the time I got home the cops were looking for me. When I walked in the house with blood on my shirt, your mama was waiting at the door. See, we were having problems at the time."

"You and Mama?"

"Yeah, we had only been married for maybe a year. Anyway, she was tired of my drinking and gambling. That night was the last straw for her. She started screaming and throwing whatever was in sight."

Eric was enthralled by the story. "She hit you?"

"Did she hit me? My head still hurt from that skillet."

"What did you do?" Eric asked, laughing.

"I slapped the shit out of your mama."

"Huh?" Eric asked.

"I didn't stutter. I slapped your mama."

"You hit Mama?" Eric stood up. He was angry. "How could you do that, Pops?"

"Easy. I was a raving alcoholic lunatic."

"What did Mama do when you slapped her?"

David smiled. "She grabbed a butcher knife and chased me all around the house. She cut my shirt off me. I still got the scars on my back."

"Oh God, stop," Eric said. He was laughing so hard it hurt.

"Your mama's crazy, boy. And while she was chasing me around the house the cops were outside in the yard on a bullhorn telling me to come out."

"Oh no," Eric said.

"Oh yeah. Believe me, I wanted to go outside really bad but I couldn't stop running long enough to open the door. Every time I ran by the front window I would yell for the cops to come inside and get me."

"So what finally happened?"

"Your mama got tired. Man, I ran out the house like Jesse Owens. The cops took me straight to jail."

"What about Mama? She cut you."

"I wasn't gon' snitch on your mama. I told the cops I got cut fighting that guy in the bar."

"Whoa, that's crazy, Pops. I never would've believed it if you didn't tell me."

"I never drank hard liquor again after that. I prayed to God for help, and your mother and I patched things up. The rest is history." David shook his head at the memory. "Boy, they don't make women like your mother anymore."

Eric nodded.

"Son, I told you that story so that you know that nobody's perfect. Not even your father."

"Marriage is crazy," Eric said.

"And hard work. Speaking of marriage, how's your boy LeBaron doing?"

Eric looked at the ground and mumbled, "Um, I guess he's alright."

"Whadda ya' mean, you guess? That's your best friend."

"We're not really speaking at the moment, Pops."

David shook his head in disgust. "Not speaking? He's your friend, not your girlfriend. What happened?"

Eric exhaled deeply. "Well, you see we uh, fell out over drugs."

David's eyes bugged. "LeBaron's on drugs too?"

"No, Pops. He's pissed at me because of what happened."

"He won't talk to you?"

"No, I won't talk to him."

"What? LeBaron is like a brother to you. You need to make that right, son."

"I will, Pops." Eric nodded. "I promise I will."

Chapter Thirty

LeBaron was uncharacteristically silent as the handsome male ultrasound technician spread a huge glob of jelly over Phoenix's belly. He didn't like the fact that he was rubbing all over his wife while she was half naked in a hospital smock, bra, and panties.

This nigga look like Blair Underwood. They don't have any female or gay ultrasound technicians in this hospital? he thought.

"How much jelly you gon' use, bruh?" he asked.

"This'll be about it." The technician smiled at Phoenix. She giggled at LeBaron's jealousy.

"I'm so nervous, LeBaron." Phoenix flinched. The jelly was cold. "I'm not sure if I want to know if it's a girl or a boy."

LeBaron squeezed her hand. "I'm excited. I can't wait to see little LeBaron Jr."

"Uh-uh," Phoenix said matter-of-factly. "If it *is* a boy, we are not naming our son LeBaron."

"Huh? Why not?" He looked up from the ultrasound screen. "What's wrong with LeBaron? That's my name."

"Nothing's wrong with it . . . if you're a car company," Phoenix deadpanned. The technician burst out laughing, smearing jelly on his smock. Phoenix strained her head toward him.

"Why do men always think the baby is going to be a boy?" Phoenix asked. The technician shrugged his shoulders as if to say "Leave me out of it."

LeBaron jumped in, trying to save face. "I don't care if it's a boy or girl, as long as it's healthy. What about Eric?" LeBaron asked.

"Now I know you're out of your mind," Phoenix said.

"Why?"

"First of all, that name is too common. And why would you name your child after a crackhead?"

The technician smiled at the comment while focusing on the screen. The ultrasound blipped, and a fuzzy black-and-white image began coming into focus.

"Well," the technician said. "Look what we have here."

LeBaron squinted. "What exactly *do* we have here?"

"It's a boy," the technician said.

"A boy!" the couple screamed. LeBaron turned and pumped his fist.

Phoenix frowned. "Calm down, Tiger Woods. We're still not naming our son after a car."

Chapter Thirty-one

Eric sighed as he eased back into the plush leather seat in first class. He felt like the weight of the world had been lifted off him. The next thing on his agenda was to go to D.C. and apologize to LeBaron.

The flight to Washington's Reagan National Airport was full. As he glanced around the first-class cabin, Eric was thankful for the empty seat next to him. He didn't feel like talking to anyone. He had too much thinking to do. Eric pulled out his journal. Lately, it had become an accessory for him, like a wallet. As he began to write, his nostrils twitched. It was a beautiful scent. He looked up, and leaning over him were two of the most perfectly formed breasts, connected to one of the most gorgeous flight attendants he had ever seen.

"Good morning, sir. My name is Africa. I'll be assisting

you today. Would you like something to snack on or drink?" she purred.

"Oh no. Thank you, I'm fine."

Her eyes narrowed and she studied his face for a moment, then said, "Okay, but if you need anything, anything, I'll be right up front, okay?"

Eric gulped as he watched her ass cheeks bounce to the front of the cabin. He recovered and tried to get back to his journal, but his mind kept going back to thoughts of nibbling on the inside of Africa's thighs.

No, he thought. *I must resist temptation. I've made too much progress. I've come too far to backslide.*

Eric's Journal

I am ready to go back home. Pop's cancer is in remission and it looks like he's going to be alright. That was a close call. God works in crazy ways. I now know that all of this was part of a larger plan to bring me closer to God. I have slacked my entire life when it comes to spirituality. God has given me so much and I have given very little in return. Hell, I don't even know what I've given. As I go back to New York, I go back with a new attitude. No more drugs. No more loose sex. Damn, I almost couldn't write that. And I am going to go to church!

"Excuse me, sir. Are you okay?" Africa asked.

Damn, why is the devil tempting me? Eric thought, and said tightly, "I'm fine. Thank you."

"Okay, if you need anyth—"

"I know," Eric cut her off. "You'll be right up front." They laughed.

Okay, keep messing with me and your legs are gonna be right up in the air. He got back to his journal.

I must conquer my addiction to women. I admit it, I can't help myself. I need help. Maybe I do need to see a therapist like LeBaron did. Hell nah! I'ma go to church.

Eric put the journal away and rested his head on a pillow propped against the window. He drifted off into sleep unaware that Africa was watching him.

Eric had slept so soundly he hadn't realized the plane had landed. He rubbed the sleep from his eyes and grabbed his carry-on.

As he exited the plane, Africa handed him an *Essence* magazine. "Sir, you forgot this," she said.

Eric was confused. It wasn't his magazine.

She winked and said, "That article you were asking about is on page one hundred."

"Oh, uh, okay. Thanks," he said. He flipped through the pages as he entered the terminal. On page one hundred a note fell out.

I'm at the Hyatt on Pennsylvania Avenue. Meet me in the bar at 5 PM. I have something for you. Africa.

Eric laughed and threw the magazine in a nearby trash can. *I don't give a damn what anybody says, the devil ain't got no horns, he got a weave.* He smiled as he pocketed the note.

Chapter Thirty-two

Eric arrived at the bar ten minutes early. He had promised himself that he was not going to hook up with Africa, but the overwhelming force of lust melted his willpower. He ordered a Captain Morgan rum and Coke and cursed himself.

I should just get up and leave.

That thought was erased as Africa glided into the restaurant. She had on a light pink Juicy Couture sweat suit. It hugged her voluptuous five-foot-eight frame like a diver's wet suit. Her perky C cups were standing at attention, thanks to excellent advances in technology. Africa's long black hair was pulled back into a long ponytail. She looked like a darker version of the R & B singer Sade, minus an inch or two of forehead. Eric tried to stand but felt like he had been punched in the stomach.

I'm going to hell, he thought. *And I'm cool with that.*

"Hello," Africa said.

"Well, hello to you too," Eric said to her chest.

"I didn't think you'd come," she said.

"I wasn't sure myself."

"Well, why did you?" She bit her bottom lip, then motioned him to follow her to a table.

"I hope to find out soon."

He couldn't take his eyes off her ass. It was shaped like a giant chocolate Valentine's Day candy heart. They sat at a table in the back of the half-full restaurant.

"So, Eric, how have you been?" she asked.

"How do you know my name?" he asked warily.

"I can't believe you don't remember me," she said, faking sadness.

Uh-oh, I hope she isn't about to tell me I'm a father.

"I used to be a Redskins cheerleader."

Eric exhaled a sigh of relief. He then searched his memory file. "Ah yeah, I remember you. How could I forget you? But you look different."

"I had shorter hair back then."

And smaller breasts.

"Shorter hair, that's right. What a small world," he said, still searching his memory file.

"I know what you're thinking." She smiled. "We've never been out on a date."

A waiter brought over a basket of bread. Africa grabbed a roll and started chewing. "Sorry," she said. "I haven't eaten all day."

Eric laughed. "I didn't think we dated because I knew I wouldn't forget someone like you." He stared at her lips, thinking that she had great mouth mechanics.

"Thank you," she said, gulping a hunk of bread.

Damn, she's hungrier than Star Jones.

Africa continued. "I had such a big crush on you back then. But you know we couldn't have relationships with the players."

"Yeah, that was a stupid rule," he said.

She grinned. "Well, looks like we're both out of the league, so to speak. So what's up?"

"You tell me." Eric's cell phone rang.

"I want to make love to you."

"Huh?" Eric cleared his throat. "Umm, I want you to make love to me too," he said, pressing the talk button.

"What's up, LeBaron?" He put a finger up to Africa as if to say "I'll be one minute." She kept stuffing the bread in her mouth.

"Thanks for returning my call," Eric said. "Look, bruh, I'm in town and I want to come over and holla at you." He paused, listening as LeBaron chewed him out.

"I know, I know," he said defensively. "But I can explain everyth—"

Africa coughed. Eric frowned at her and continued his conversation. A few seconds later, her coughing grew louder and more intense. Eric glowered at her and went back to talking. All of a sudden Africa grabbed her throat and started violently choking, knocking all the plates and glasses off the table. They crashed to the floor, shards of glass and china flying in all directions. She then kicked the table, turning it over too. The entire restaurant fell silent. The customers were frozen, staring at Africa gag. None of them offered to help.

"What the—?" Eric dropped his cell phone. Africa had fallen backward in her chair. She was in a panic, tears running down her face. Eric ran behind Africa and snatched her up, wrapping his arms from behind her to start doing the Heimlich. He squeezed while she heaved. After a few more squeezes, a huge hunk of bread flew out of her mouth.

"Jesus, are you okay?" Eric asked, picking the chair up for her.

Africa struggled to catch her breath. "Oh my God!" She fell back into the chair. "I thought I was going to die."

People in the restaurant were still staring at them. The manager came over. Eric waved him off.

This is some crazy shit, he thought. He was looking around for Ashton Kutcher, thinking maybe he was being "Punked."

He noticed then that Africa was staring at him very intensely. She had a weird look on her blotchy face.

"What's wrong?" he asked.

"You saved my life." She started crying and got up and hugged him tight. "You saved my life. I knew God brought you back into my life for a reason."

"Huh? What? Back *into* your life?" Eric began feeling

nervous. Something was off . . . *Uh-oh! Fatal attraction.* He backed away carefully, trying to get out of her embrace.

"What's wrong?" she asked, clinging to him.

"Stay right here," he ordered her. "I'll be right back."

"Where are you going?" she pleaded, wiping tears off her face. "Don't leave me."

"I'm . . . uh . . ." He grasped for a good lie. "I'm going to the front desk to see if there is a doctor."

"I'm fine," Africa said, inching toward him. "I don't need a doctor. All I need is you. You saved my life."

She has lost her damn mind, he thought. The expression of the onlookers at their tables told him they were thinking the same thing.

"No, stay right here. I'll be right back." Eric grabbed a glass of water from a nearby table and gave it to her. "Drink this," he offered.

"Thank you, sweetheart," Africa said obediently. She watched him walk out of the dining area. Eric hurried to the front desk, aware that she was watching him ask the concierge a question. The concierge pointed toward the front lobby. Eric nodded his head and looked at Africa. He pointed at the front door as if to say, "The doctor is in there. I'll be right back." She waved. Eric waved good-bye.

Chapter Thirty-three

Later that night at LeBaron's house, he and Eric laughed like old times. Eric was really animated as he told the story about Africa.

"And you just left her?" LeBaron asked, opening his liquor cabinet.

"Hell, yeah. Right at the damn table," Eric said with a laugh. "She had stalker written all over her phat ass."

LeBaron poured two drinks. "E, your ass is crazy. You haven't changed a bit."

Eric held up a finger. "Ah, but that's where you're wrong, grasshopper."

"Do tell." LeBaron was skeptical.

"I am in the process of a mental and spiritual rebirth."

"What!" LeBaron almost spit out his drink. "Now I know you must be on drugs." As soon as he said it, he wished he could take the comment back.

"You got something to say?" Eric said testily.

"I just said it." LeBaron stood up. He had an equally angry glare. "Now that it's out there . . . I didn't appreciate the way you bugged the hell out when I came to New York."

Eric's anger melted away at the comment. He was still embarrassed about that. "I know—"

"Forget that I know shit," LeBaron cut him off. "That ain't enough. I'm your friend. I've been with you through mad shit. I left my damn pregnant wife, my sick pregnant wife, to come see about you and you act out like that? Phoenix is really hating your ass right now. That's the real reason she is in the room and hasn't come out to see you."

Eric was silent.

"You have been really foul. I don't preach to you. You're a grown-ass man and too old to be acting like this. I haven't spoken to you in months. Nobody knows what the hell happened to you. You don't treat your friends—no, better yet—you don't treat your family like that."

Eric sat there staring at the wall.

"You don't have anything to say?"

"I'm sorry."

"That's it?"

"LeBaron, you are like a brother to me, and all I can say is I'm sorry. I'm sorry that I upset Phoenix. I'm sorry . . . I'm sorry . . . I'm sorry . . . It wasn't me talking. It was the coke. Now if you don't want to be my friend any-more, brother, I understand." Eric stood, put the drink on the coffee table, and headed for the door.

LeBaron stared at him for a few seconds, then blocked

the door. He gave Eric a pound on the back and hugged him. "That's good enough for me."

"Thanks, LeBaron." They walked back to the couch.

"So tell me about this mental and spiritual rebirth."

"You've known me for a long time, right, LB?"

"Damn near ten years."

"Have you ever known me to talk about God?"

"Only when you say 'Goddamn, that's a fine-ass woman,' " LeBaron cracked.

"I'm serious. A lot has happened to me in the last few months. I got fired, acquired a drug habit, fell in and out of love."

"Fell in love?" LeBaron laughed. "What's his name?"

Eric stared at him like he was crazy. "Quit playing. Remember Eden, the anchor I was telling you about?"

"The one whose ass left you shocked and awed?" LeBaron smiled.

"That would be her. We got tight, real tight, and we never even had sex."

"You're lying." LeBaron was unconvinced.

"I lie, but I don't lie about that. We never had sex, and just when I was about to get serious and settle down with her, she dropped a nigga like a bad habit."

"A woman dissed you? The most valuable playa?"

"Real funny." Eric smirked. "Can't you see I'm devastated?"

"Uh . . . yeah." LeBaron's expression changed, and he looked intently into Eric's eyes.

"I even started going to church with her."

"Church? This is too much." LeBaron walked back to the liquor cabinet. "I got to get me another drink."

"Get me one too. Yeah, I went to church, but that ain't even the half. Pops almost died."

"What?"

"Yeah, he had cancer."

"And you didn't tell me?" LeBaron was getting angry.

"I was messed up, man. I didn't know if I was coming or going. I had to work that out for myself."

"How is he?"

"The cancer is in remission. He's gaining his weight back, but that chemo got his head smoother than Jordan's."

"I bet he still talking smack too, huh?"

"You know it. But now I know why all of this happened."

"Why?"

"God was talking to me."

"How do you figure that?" LeBaron handed Eric a drink.

"I was in full self-destruct mode," he said, sipping from the glass. "I was doing *whatever* I wanted to do, *whenever* I wanted to do it, and *how many* times I wanted to do it. Money, hos, coke, and clothes. Hear me? I ain't give a damn. Then my father gets sick. I almost checked out fo' real."

"I didn't know it was that bad," LeBaron said.

"Shit, me either. That's what coke will do to you. I

should be dead right now. God gave me a chance and I'm not going to blow it on no blow."

"I'm glad to hear that. So how you dealing with your habit?"

"Cold turkey. I haven't done coke in months and have no desire to. I lost too much. I'm just glad I got money."

"What you gon' do?"

"Get back on TV."

"How?"

"My agent got me an audition."

"Where?"

"ESPN."

"That's great. That's some real good news. I have some good news too."

"What?"

"Phoenix and I are having a boy."

"Congratulations." Eric hugged his best friend. "I better be the Goddaddy."

"Of course."

"Hey man, go and get Phoenix," Eric said.

LeBaron made a face. "I don't know about that."

"C'mon, man. I need to apologize to her too."

"A'right," LeBaron said. "I'll be right back."

A few minutes later Phoenix stood at the door. Her long hair was in a ponytail. She was wearing a cute peach-colored maternity dress. She was also wearing a frown.

Eric got up and walked over to her. "Phoenix, you look fantastic."

"Thank you." She waddled over and LeBaron helped her down to the couch.

"What's up, Eric?" she said, slightly irritated.

"I know that you know." He paused to clear his throat. "I've had some problems, letting the temptations of the world get the best of me."

Phoenix was nonplussed.

Eric continued. "I just want to say I'm sorry to you. You guys are like family to me and I let you down and I hurt you. Can you forgive me?"

"Eric, I don't hold anything against you. You're a grown man. I just don't want LeBaron getting mixed up in your mess. Hey, you are family and families have issues, but at the end of the day we got to love our family."

He smiled and hugged her. "Honesty. That's what I always loved about you, P."

"I just have one question," Phoenix said.

"Shoot."

"What ever happened to your anchor girlfriend?"

Eric looked at LeBaron, who threw up his hands. "I didn't tell her."

Phoenix smiled and kept at it. "You know, the one whose ass left you shocked and awed."

"Uh . . ." Eric cleared his throat again.

Phoenix arched her eyebrow. "Well?"

Chapter Thirty-four

The news business is such an emotional roller coaster. One moment, it has you feeling like you are on top of the world. Moments later, it could have you wishing that you were never born. That irony is what Eden was thinking while she was being driven home from work. She was on the phone with Richard Weiss, her agent. He had some distressing news to share with her. Richard had just hung up with David Denson, the executive producer of *America This Morning* and Eden's boss.

"How upset is he?" Eden asked.

"Let's just say that he's not in a good mood," Richard said. "He's been getting his ass chewed by the network about the low ratings."

"And that's my fault?" Eden said.

"Of course not. Nobody's blaming you. But you know how the brass is. Always ready to shoot from the hip."

"So what does that mean for me?"

"I won't lie to you. If the ratings don't improve, they might make a switch."

"A switch?" Eden yelled. "Damn, I've only been on the show for a few months."

Richard cut her off. "I know, I know. Calm down, Eden. Nobody's doing anything yet."

Eden sighed. "Richard, the network isn't so fun after all."

"I told you that, Eden. The pressure is enormous, but let's stay positive. C'mon, you're the one who is always talking about faith."

"That's me, old faithful." Eden hung up the phone.

They could just cut me off like that? Now I know how Eric must have felt.

I should have just stayed at the local station. At least there the ratings were high. Maybe they'll take me back if this doesn't work out. How could I have been so naive about the network?

Chapter Thirty-five

After two days in D.C., Eric was excited to be heading back to New York. He felt good about patching things up with LeBaron. As he settled into the plush first-class cabin chair of the Amtrak Acela train, he reflected on the days ahead. He'd been gone nearly three months and was eager to get his life back on track. The first order of business was to get a job. Eric had plenty of money in the bank, but he still had the itch to be on TV. He was too young to retire, plus he didn't want his legacy to be one of failure. Plenty of anchors had come back from worse offenses. Besides, his prospects were looking bright. His agent had scheduled an audition with ESPN for the coming Friday, three days away. Eric was a little rusty but felt up for the challenge. The audition was a lucky break because after the news of his firing spread throughout the close-knit television industry, the odds were that he'd never work in New York again.

His next order of business would be to apologize to Eden. He still had high hopes that they could reconcile.

It was a three-hour train ride back to New York, so Eric had plenty of time to kill. He thumbed through the television sections of the city papers to catch up on the latest industry buzz. He noticed in the *Daily News* that his old sports job had been taken by one of ESPN's top anchors. A white anchor.

I see ABC ain't hiring no mo' Negroes, Eric mused, smirking. *I must be auditioning for his old job.*

There was another item about a well-known local weatherman busted for a DWI. The New York press was brutal. Eric knew that firsthand.

He picked up the *Post*, and a blurb about *America This Morning Weekend Edition* caught his attention. The article said that the ratings were down 32 percent and there was speculation that changes were going to be made. His heart sank.

Further down in the article it mentioned Eden by name. The writer cited sources that said she might be reassigned or, worse, canned.

I hope she's okay. I have to call her as soon as I get home. Then he remembered that Eden had changed her number. He kept reading. There was also an asterisk by her name indicating there was another item about her on the *Post*'s infamous Page Six. Eric damn near tore the pages flipping back to the section. He scanned through the half dozen or so items until he saw her name in bold.

"What?" he said, throwing the paper down. He couldn't believe his eyes. A few heads in the first-class car turned and scowled at him, but he paid them no mind. He grabbed the paper and read it again, his heart rate increasing.

Why is Eden with this clown? he thought derisively, looking at the photo of Eden with another man. He stared at the newspaper during the rest of the train ride and the entire cab ride from Penn Station. It began to eat him up inside.

Eric was glad he had maid service. His apartment looked as if he had never left. Jenny, his Dominican housekeeper, had even stocked his refrigerator with his favorite snack, Heineken. Eric frowned. *Got to get rid of that shit.* He reached behind the beer and grabbed a bottle of grape juice. He then threw the *New York Post* with the photo of Eden and Derek Outlaw, the Giants' newest wide receiver, on the dinette table.

They should have put a headline on it that read "Beauty and the Beast." I can't believe she's dating his ugly ass. She's probably sexing him too. Nah, he's always talking about abstinence. I bet his ass is lying. He can't treat her the way I would.

No doubt about it, Eric was jealous. Derek Outlaw was a big NFL star blessed with an even bigger contract.

"I thought Eden didn't like football players," he exclaimed as he threw the paper in the trash.

Bitch.

Eric plopped down onto his couch and clicked on the television. *That ain't right, E. She doesn't deserve to be called that. Whatever, I hope she's happy.* He paused a few seconds to think about the newspaper article. *The bitch damn sho' looked happy.*

Chapter Thirty-six

It had been two days since Eden's conversation with Richard, and she was still upset. She had put up a good front at work, but home was a different matter.

"It's just rumors, Eden," Derek said, stroking her chin. "Baby, I deal with the press all the time." His words were comforting, but the tears still fell from her eyes. The gossip had even started showing up on the Internet. When Eden had confronted her executive producer, David was evasive.

"Spineless," she said, accepting the tissue.

Eden was glad that Derek was there to console her. She had been dating Derek Outlaw for the last three months. Eden had met Derek at an awards function for the United Negro College Fund. He was six foot three and had the physique of a lean bodybuilder. He wasn't the most attractive brother she had dated, in fact he wasn't good-looking at all, but Eden never really went for pretty boys. Well, except for Eric.

"I feel betrayed by David," Eden continued. "He sat me down and told me ABC was committed to me."

"I heard the same thing before I got traded to New York," Derek said. Eden cut her eyes at him.

"Ooops, sorry," he said, not meaning to imply that she would soon be jettisoned.

"I busted my ass to get to the network." Eden threw her hands in the air. "And this is what I get? Well, the network isn't all that it's cracked up to be. At least they could have the decency to tell me to my face that they want to get rid of me."

Derek wrapped Eden in his muscular arms and looked deep into her eyes. "Well, beautiful, look at the bright side."

Eden smirked. "What bright side?"

"Well, I just got a seven-million-dollar bonus."

"And what does that have to do with me?"

"If ABC doesn't work out, you'll never have to work again."

Eden felt like the wind had been knocked out of her. It had been only three months, but she was starting to fall in love with Derek. He was so romantic and generous to her, but what Eden loved the most was the fact that he was a devout Christian. And to top it off, he was committed to abstinence, at least until he got married. And in Eden's mind, Derek was certainly starting to look like marriage material. He seemed to be the exact opposite of Eric.

Chapter Thirty-seven

Reverend Francois gave Cheryl, his secretary, a perplexed look as she announced the name of his 11 AM appointment.

"What did um"—he looked down at the name in his day planner again—"Mr. Swift say he wanted?"

"He just said that he wanted to talk," Cheryl answered.

"That right? His name sounds familiar."

"He's a sports anchor on channel seven."

"Ah, that's it." Reverend Francois snapped his fingers. "He used to play for the Redskins." *And he recently got fired from his job in a drug scandal*, he recalled. *I wonder what he wants.* A lifelong sports fanatic, Reverend Francois was always up on sports stars and sportscasters.

The minister stood and walked toward the door. "Okay, send him in."

Dispensing with formalities, he reached out and gave Eric a pound and a hug. After the men shared pleasantries,

Eric sat down across from the young minister. He had a nervous look on his face.

Reverend Francois looked him up and down, concerned. "Are you okay, brother?"

Eric kept his eyes on the floor. "I'm okay, um . . . brother? Or should I call you . . ." Eric scratched the back of his head. "What do I call you?"

The pastor smiled. "Call me Joshua."

"Okay, Joshua. A friend of mine . . ." Eric cleared his throat. "I mean my coworker Eden."

"Eden Alexander?" Joshua asked.

"Yes," Eric said. "She's a member here. Anyway, she took me to hear you preach earlier this year at the Garden. Your sermon was incredible."

Joshua nodded.

"What you said was so amazing," Eric continued. "I was really feeling what you were saying. It was the first time I connected to a pastor's message."

"I appreciate that. That's very kind of you."

"I have always been skeptical about preachers, but I could tell that you were different. For one thing you were the youngest pastor up there." Eric laughed. "Those older ministers looked a lil' upset with you."

Joshua smiled. "You know, I have to admit that it's real hard sometimes."

"I feel you," Eric agreed. "Since we're about the same age and we shared similar experiences, with me being in the league and on TV and with you being in the music industry and everything, I feel like you could give me some advice."

"That's what I'm here for, brother."

"See, Joshua, I've really been struggling with my faith lately, and ever since I moved here from D.C. I have been just ridiculous." Eric shook his head for emphasis. "I mean *really* ridiculous."

Joshua smiled. He remembered the days when he was really ridiculous too.

"Can I be frank with you, Joshua?"

"Of course."

"I've had some real bad luck lately. My father is battling cancer. I lost my job, lost the woman that I love. I've been dabbling in drugs and I just can't seem to get a handle on my life. I've prayed about it, cried about it, and I tried to do right. But the bad shit—sorry, I mean bad stuff—just keeps happening. I thought that when you prayed and made a sincere effort to change your life, God was supposed to bless you."

Joshua stroked his chin. "Are you still breathing?"

Eric smirked. "Of course I am."

"Then God is blessing you."

Eric stared at the preacher.

"Your first mistake is believing that you pray to get blessed. Your purpose is to glorify God because God is holy and great. Don't just praise God because you feel it's your duty or you fear God's wrath and punishment. Pray to and praise God because of your love and gratitude."

Reverend Francois got up, walked over to his window,

and looked outside for a few seconds. "Look, Eric, I'm not about to tell you that I know why God has put these obstacles in your path, but I will tell you that God has an infinite variety of ways to test our faith. As mere humans, we are not advanced enough to understand the reason why. God tested Adam and Eve, Job and Abraham. Tests reveal your character. Let me ask you a question, Eric. Before these calamities, were you calling on God?"

Eric thought for a second. "Honestly? No."

"If you take one step to God, God will take two steps to you. God needed to get your attention."

"Well, he certainly got it." Eric sighed.

"I went through a similar situation with my music career. I was living foul. Drugs, women, whatever! I did it . . . three times. I thought I was invincible, and just when I was at the top, it all came crashing down. People around me started dying. See, I was rolling with grimy cats who were really doing it fo' real. Cats were stealing from me, the label was trying to jerk me on my royalties. My last album went triple copper. I was damn near broke over crazy lawsuits, and to top it off, I was strung out on alcohol, coke, and weed. I almost died. I was ready to die. But Jesus saved me, gave me a new start. Jesus can do that for you too, Eric."

"But why do we have to go through these changes? Why does your life have to fall apart? God could just tell us to do right."

"God has told us to do right. God has told us that a million trillion times. But Eric, we all know that humans only respond to tough love. Dig this, out of the worst can come the best."

"I'm not following you."

"I'll ask you another question. What was the worst thing to ever happen in the history of the world?"

Eric raised an eyebrow. "Let me think. Slavery?"

Joshua shook his head no.

"Don't tell me. The Holocaust."

"Not even close."

Eric threw his hands up. "Well, I don't know. What? Was it the Knicks getting blasted by Jordan to get to the finals? I know, Montell Jordan's last album?"

"Nah, Eric, this is serious business." Joshua was stern. "The worst thing to ever happen in the history of the world was Jesus Christ dying on the cross."

Eric nodded.

"Now get this," Joshua went on. "The best thing that ever happened to the world was Jesus dying on the cross."

"Huh?" Now Eric was confused. "How could that be?"

"Wait," Joshua cut him off. "Jesus died so that we could live, and that's the best thing that has ever happened to mankind. So you see, out of the worst of times can come the best of times."

"I've never thought about it like that. That's deep."

Joshua nodded. "God is very deep."

"So maybe there is hope for a poor old sinner like me?"

"Eric, as long as you're still breathing, there is always hope for a poor old sinner."

Chapter Thirty-eight

"LeBaron!" Phoenix screamed.

"What the fuck?" LeBaron jumped. He'd been half asleep in the living room watching a History Channel episode on the Black Panthers. "What's wrong, baby?" he yelled over his shoulder. *She probably wants some damn ice cream.*

"LeBaron, get your *black* ass in here!"

"Uh-oh." He bolted out of the chair and smashed his bare foot on the coffee table leg. "Ouch . . . damn," he moaned while rubbing his foot. LeBaron limped into the bedroom and froze.

"Oh my God," he blurted. "What happened?"

"My water broke," Phoenix cried. A huge wet stain soaked nearly half the bed.

"Y-Y-Your water broke?" LeBaron stuttered.

That mattress cost damn near a thousand dollars, he thought but dared not speak.

"Can't you see that?" Phoenix was hysterical. "I need to get to the hospital now."

"The hospital . . . right . . . right . . . the hospital." LeBaron was dazed. He looked around the bedroom. "Uh, where's the number?"

"What number? Call a damn ambulance!" Phoenix screamed. That jolted him back to reality.

"Right." He raced to the phone and dialed 911. He then helped Phoenix put on a fresh pair of warm-up pants and lifted her out of bed.

"LeBaron, I'm scared. It's too early. I'm only seven and a half months."

He helped her into her top. "Baby, it's gon' be alright." He caressed her face.

"Ow." She grabbed her belly.

"What? Contractions?"

She nodded.

In a matter of minutes, the ambulance was there. After the EMTs loaded Phoenix in the back, they sped off with sirens blaring. LeBaron was nervous as he sat in the back of the ambulance but hid his anxiety. He smiled at Phoenix and held her hand. As the ambulance pulled up to the hospital, he again questioned if he was ready for fatherhood. *Got no choice*, he thought. *It's happening. It's time to be a man.*

"Get out of the way!" the paramedic yelled. A young man with his arm in a cast barely managed to dodge the gurney, nearly catching his foot in the wheels. The Neonatal Intensive Care Unit team was waiting for Phoenix at the emergency room doors along with Dr. Peterson, her ob-gyn.

"How are you doing, Phoenix?" Dr. Peterson asked.

"I . . . I . . . uh." Phoenix gasped. She tried to answer but she felt like a python was wrapped around her stomach.

"She's in a lot of pain," LeBaron said, holding her hand. The paramedics were moving Phoenix so fast he was almost being dragged.

"Hold on, Phoenix. We'll get you through this," Dr. Peterson assured her, keeping up with the team.

The NICU team wheeled her into the OB ward and immediately went to work. One nurse checked her vital signs while another quickly hooked her up to a monitor.

"We are going to measure your contractions and check the baby's heart rate, okay?" the nurse explained. Phoenix nodded.

The nurses scooted LeBaron out of the room so they could finish their checks. He paced just outside the door and tried to eavesdrop on their conversation. After a few minutes, the nurses allowed LeBaron to return to the room.

A half hour later, the nurse checked the printout and shot Dr. Peterson a serious look. "Heart rate is falling."

LeBaron had a panicked look on his face. Phoenix was in too much pain to even hear the nurse.

"Keep a close eye on that heart rate," Dr. Peterson ordered. She then turned to Phoenix and LeBaron. "If the baby's heart rate keeps falling, we may have to perform an emergency C-section," Dr. Peterson said. LeBaron nodded.

"Oh God! It hurts," Phoenix moaned. LeBaron squeezed her hand tighter. Phoenix was dilated to six centimeters. She needed to be at least ten centimeters to push the baby out. It was going to be a long, painful afternoon and the NICU doctor needed to explain what was going to happen.

"When the baby comes out we have to take it immediately. You won't be able to hold it," he said.

"Huh?" LeBaron snapped.

"I can't hold my baby?" Phoenix cried.

"I'm sorry," the doctor said with a concerned look. "We have to make sure that the baby can breathe on its own."

"Ow!" Phoenix clutched her belly. "The pain . . ." The couple had vowed to have a natural delivery but the pain was almost too much.

"Okay," Dr. Peterson said. "We have to make a decision soon. If you dilate any more, we won't be able to give you an epidural."

Phoenix and LeBaron looked at each other.

"It's your decision," LeBaron said. "I'm here with you no matter what."

Phoenix took a deep breath. "Don't give me one."

"Are you sure?" LeBaron asked.

She cut her eyes at him.

"Okay, okay," he said. "I'll be right by your side, baby. Every step of the way."

Chapter Thirty-nine

"Puhleeeease, Eric, lemme come over," Claudia purred into the phone. She was almost begging. "I'll do whatever you want me to do." Her voice was so melodious it was intoxicating.

Eric frowned at the phone as he held it inches away from his ear. "Not tonight, baby. I'ma little jet-lagged," he lied. *Damn . . . I really could use some head tonight. No, E, stay strong.*

It was taking a tremendous amount of willpower for Eric to say no to her. Because when it came to head, Claudia was at the head of the class. She was the headmistress, a headliner. In short, Claudia was headstrong.

"Look, baby, I'm in a different place right now and I'm not trying to get down like that."

"Huh? Eric, that don't even sound like you." Claudia was getting testy. "You got another bitch coming over?"

"No, no, no, I'm chilling, trying to get myself to-gether."

"Getting yourself together? How?"

"Spiritually."

Claudia paused and smacked her lips. "You didn't seem too spiritual the last time we had sex."

Click. Eric hung up the phone on her. *Bitches.*

He walked over to the closet and searched for a suit to wear to his anchor audition at ESPN the next day. He ran his hands over the row of expensive suits. When the phone rang he ignored it. His eyes focused on a favorite outfit. *Ah, this one will do.* It was a blue three-button Armani suit. He matched it with a solid white shirt with French cuffs and a blue and red striped Hermès tie. Eric held the outfit up to the mirror, thinking, *I am going to blow their asses away tomorrow.*

He set the alarm clock. Eric wanted to wake up early to avoid taking any risks with his second chance. He knelt down at the side of the bed and reflected.

Thank you, God, for this opportunity. I really need this break. I feel like my life depends on it. I need you to walk with me tomorrow. What did Joshua say? Out of the worst of times can come the best of times. I need your strength. You've been bet-ter to me than I deserve. I promise you I will not mess th—"

The phone rang again. Eric was upset and yanked it off the cradle. "Look, Claudia," he barked.

"Eric?" His mother cut him off. Her tone was stern.

"Oh, hey, Ma. I was just—"

"Eric!" Shirley snapped. "Your daddy is dead."

Eric felt like someone slapped him. He was silent for a couple of seconds. "What do you mean Pops is dead? What happened?"

"He had a heart attack," Shirley sobbed.

"A heart attack? No, Mama, no. Daddy can't be dead."

"Yes, son. He's gone. I had just come back from the grocery store. When I walked in the house, something felt strange. I called out for your daddy and there was no answer. I walked in the living room and there he was, sitting in his chair, dead. Oh Lord," she moaned. "I don't know what I'm gon' do without that man."

"Mama, is there anybody there with you?"

"Yeah. Mo' Jessie's here."

"I'm catching the first plane down there."

"No, son, nothing you can do here right now. I need you to do something for me first."

"Anything, Mama."

"Go tell your brother that your daddy is dead."

The news of David's death knocked the wind out of Eric. After he hung up the phone, he stood in a daze. Then he threw the phone at the wall. It exploded into a half dozen pieces. He desperately stomped back and forth in the living room. His heart was racing. He could barely breathe.

"No . . . no . . . no. Pops can't be dead." He banged his fist against the wall. Pain shot through his hands but he ignored it. Defeated, Eric fell back against the wall and slowly slid down to the floor and cried.

A heart attack? But he beat cancer. I don't understand. How could he have a heart attack? "I just spoke to him yesterday," he said in complete disbelief. Eric felt betrayed, like the floor had fallen from under him.

God, is this some kind of cruel twisted joke? I did everything I could do. I changed my life. I quit drugs, I quit drinking, left the women alone. And you do this to me? It ain't fair. It ain't fair.

Eric was mad. He got up off the floor, walked over to his bar, and poured himself a shot glass of Courvoisier. He downed it in one swig. The warm liquor burned his throat. He grabbed the bottle and sat down on the couch and poured another drink.

"Fuck it. You don't care. I don't care," he declared, raising the shot glass to the air in a mock toast.

After two more shots he wobbled into the downstairs bathroom to take a piss. After flushing the toilet, Eric opened his medicine cabinet to get some soap.

"Oh *shiii*," he slurred. "What do we have here?"

It was a small glassine bag filled with cocaine. Eric thought he had gotten rid of all the little stashes he'd hidden around the house. He grabbed a hand mirror and rushed back into his living room and spread out the cocaine into thick white lines. He rolled a crisp twenty-dollar bill into a tight straw and inhaled three lines quickly and deeply. Seconds later the coke soaked his brain and engulfed him in a wave of euphoria. Eric closed his eyes, leaning back into the sofa with a deeply satisfied smile.

Chapter Forty

"Just take deep breaths, baby. It's gon' be okay." LeBaron patted his wife's shoulder, trying to reassure her.

"Ow! Don't tell me to breathe." Phoenix was hunched over, arms wrapped around her belly. "I knew I should have taken the epidural. Ow! It's all your fault."

"But baby, you—"

"Goddammit, LeBaron. I don't care what I said." She cut him off. "You should have made me take it."

LeBaron closed his eyes. *God please let this baby come soon or we gon' have a birth and a death.* He gently caressed her shoulder.

"Get your damn hands off me."

He calmly and slowly removed his hand from her shoulder. *Jesus, help me, I'm about to curse out my pregnant wife.*

Phoenix had been in labor for four hours. It had been

four hours of constant pain for both her and LeBaron. His head was hurting from the constant abuse. He had no idea his wife could be so mean. *She said she wasn't ever having sex with me again*, he thought. *She can't be serious.*

As he stood next to her, daydreaming about going to court for spousal abuse, Phoenix's elbow smashed into his groin.

"Ow!" he screamed. It was a high-pitched scream. "What the fuck?"

"Get the doctor," Phoenix yelled.

LeBaron limped to the door and hollered for Dr. Peterson. She came racing in and checked Phoenix.

"You're at ten centimeters. Looks like you're ready."

"Oh God, it damn sure feels like it," Phoenix gasped.

"I want you to take a breath and push while I count to ten, okay?"

Phoenix nodded.

Dr. Peterson counted to ten.

"Okay, let's do it again."

"Ahh! LeBaron, I hate you," Phoenix screamed at her husband. Her face was bathed in sweat.

He fake-smiled at her. *Trust me, I hate you too, baby.*

"Oh my God. I'm ripping . . . it's burning . . ." she yelled, nearly out of breath.

LeBaron grimaced.

After about twenty minutes Dr. Peterson smiled. "I see the head. And look at all that hair."

LeBaron was so nervous he was about to faint.

Once the head was out a nurse suctioned the nose and mouth.

"Come on, one more push, Phoenix," Dr. Peterson coached.

"Ahh! Ahh! Ahh!" and out popped the baby along with a whole lot of other stuff. LeBaron almost threw up.

Dr. Peterson quickly cut the umbilical cord. The baby let out a wail. "Well," she said. "Looks like you two have a baby boy."

"Little LeBaron." The proud father smiled.

"I . . . I . . . told you," Phoenix gasped for breath. "I am *not* naming my child LeBaron."

Chapter Forty-one

Eric's phone had been ringing off the hook for the last hour and a half, but he didn't hear it. He was too wasted. It was the combination of his two-way pager vibrating and the ringing of his cell phone along with his house phone that finally jarred him awake.

"What?" he growled into the phone.

"Where the hell are you?" It was Martin, his agent.

"Huh?" Eric ran his hand over his face, trying to rub the sleep out. "What's wrong?" He looked at the clock but his vision was blurry.

"Don't tell me you forgot," Martin snapped.

Silence.

"Eric, the audition."

"Damn!" Eric blurted. "What time is it?" He looked at the clock again. The time came into focus. He had overslept by three hours.

"Too late, that's what time it is." Martin was irate. "I can't believe you overslept. Do you know how long they waited for you?"

Eric sat up in the bed and smacked his lips. *Damn, tastes like somebody took a dump in my mouth.*

"Can you reschedule? I had some bad news."

"Hell, no!" Martin screamed. "Don't you understand? This is it. No more chances. You're done. Look, Eric, I don't know what the hell is going on in your life, but you need to seek professional help. I can't do anything else for you." The call waiting on Eric's phone beeped.

He cut Martin off. "Hold on," he said, clicking over. "Hello?"

"Hi, son."

"Hi, Mama. Hold on a second while I get off the other line." Eric clicked back over.

"Kiss my ass, Martin," Eric exploded. "You don't fire me, I fire you. I told your blood-sucking cracker ten-percenter ass that I had some bad news." He slammed the phone so hard it almost broke.

Eric clicked back over to his mother. "Mama, I'm back."

"Are you going to see your brother today?"

Eric sighed and rubbed his hand on his forehead. "Yes, Mama. I'm getting up now."

Chapter Forty-two

"Empty your pockets!" the muscular corrections officer ordered the long line of visitors.

Eric's heart had been racing like the U.S. Olympic hundred-meter relay team ever since he entered the imposing gray stone penitentiary. He had a nervous tick and kept looking over his shoulder, eyes darting.

"Lord help me," he mumbled, placing the contents of his pockets on the X-ray conveyor belt. As he walked through the metal detector, a red light flashed and an alarm beeped. The guard eyed him hard. The German shepherd he was holding barked.

Puhleez, God, don't let me have any drugs on me. Eric fumbled with his pockets until the guard pointed at his watch. "Ooops, sorry," Eric apologized.

Eric cringed every time he heard the loud clank of the iron cell door. The very thorough strip search, complete with ass and crotch grope, didn't help his frayed nerves. It was like he was stuck in the late seventies after-school special "Scared Straight." While Eric took a seat in the visiting room, he avoided looking any of the hardened criminals in the eye.

The man trying to keep us down my ass, he thought. *By the looks of them, some of these niggas need to be in jail.*

Sing Sing was one of the oldest and toughest prisons in New York State. Located in the tiny town of Ossining, it was less than a two-hour drive from Manhattan but could have been on another planet. Cold and bleak, Sing Sing was a place where not only men died but also their thoughts and dreams. It was the last stop for many of the country's most notorious criminals, like Albert Fish, Julius and Ethel Rosenberg, and . . . Sean Swift? Eric's younger brother was currently in the fourteenth month of a three- to five-year bid for drug possession. It could have been a lot worse if Eric hadn't secured one of the most expensive criminal lawyers to defend Sean. The high-priced mouth-piece managed to get the charges knocked down to posses-sion even though Sean was caught red-handed with three kilos of pure uncut cocaine, not to mention the pound of chronic. Even though Sean was always a hard-ass, the im-prisonment devastated the family, especially David. Eric had yet to visit his little brother but he had to break the news of their father's death in person. He was lost in thought when Sean appeared standing over him.

"Eric?" Sean said, surprised. "You the last cat I ex-pected to see."

"What's up, little brother?" Eric reached out to hug him.

"I'm good." Sean held his head up high and looked Eric in the eye. It was a look one could perfect only in the pen.

Eric sized him up. "I'd say, with your buff ass." He play-punched him in the arm.

"Got to bulk up to keep these gorillas off a nigga." Sean smiled. He sat down in a plastic chair facing his brother.

Eric sneezed. His eyes were wet and red.

"You got a cold?" Sean asked.

"No, sinuses messed up."

Sean looked over his shoulder to see if anyone was listening. "Guess what?"

Eric was intrigued. "What?"

"I'm out in three months."

"What?" Eric blurted out. A guard turned to see what the commotion was about.

"Calm down," Sean said. "You in prison, not on the corner."

"Sorry, bruh," Eric whispered. "Three months? That's great. How in the hell that happen?"

"Good behavior."

"You?"

"Can you believe it?" Sean smiled. "I'm sick of these niggas."

"Mama know?" Eric asked.

"No. It's gon' be a surprise."

"Need a place to stay?"

"Nah, I'm going back to Atlanta."

Eric nodded. "I think that's a good thing."

"Unless Pops start tripping," Sean added. "You know how he is."

Eric was silent.

"Yo, what's up, E? You don't look like yourself. You ain't cracked a joke yet. And anyway, what are you doing here? You said you weren't coming to see me in jail."

"Pops is dead," Eric deadpanned.

"Huh?" Sean was stunned.

Eric stared at the floor.

"What? How? Mama told me he beat the cancer. I just spoke to him the other day."

"Heart attack," Eric said, fighting back tears.

"Damn." Sean rubbed both his hands on his face. "When?"

"A couple of days ago."

"And you're just now telling me?" Sean was angry.

"Um . . . I lost your number. What the fuck you expect me to do, call you?" Eric countered. "Besides, this is some shit I had to tell you in person."

Sean thought about it for a moment. "Yeah, I guess you're right."

"I know I'm right."

"How's Mama taking it?" Sean asked, concerned.

"Terrible. Aunt Joyce and Terry are staying with her until I can get down there."

"Tell her I love her," Sean said.

"Of course."

"Damn," Sean cursed. "They ain't gon' let me out of here for the funeral either."

Eric shook his head. "I know, but don't worry, I'll take care of Mama. At least she'll know that you'll be home soon."

"Damn, I ain't get a chance to tell him I love him. When we spoke the other day we ended up arguing over Tayja."

"He knew you loved him."

"I don't think I ever told him, though."

Eric couldn't say anything.

"This is too fucked up, E. I gotta go." Sean started to rise, but Eric grabbed his arm.

He paused in an attempt to gather his words. "I have to share something with you, Sean."

"What?"

Eric scooted his chair up. "I'm sorry for not coming to see you."

"Bruh, don't even."

Eric wouldn't let him finish. "No, man, that shit was foul. We family. It's just I feel like it's my fault that you're locked up here like an animal."

"I'm a grown-ass man, Eric. I can't put that on you."

"But I introduced you to the lifestyle. The cars, the women, the drugs. Hell, I introduced you to the cats who got you busted." Tears started to fall from Eric's eyes. "Little brother, I'm sorry."

Sean reached his hand out and squeezed Eric's shoulder. "E, I've been thug life'n like Tupac since high school, so I was always one fuckup away from the pen anyway. Don't sweat this. If I wasn't here I would be dead. This was God's plan."

A half-smile crossed his older brother's lips.

"I have some advice for you, big brother," Sean whispered.

"You? Advice for me?"

"Yeah, lay off them drugs. That shit is going to destroy you."

Eric cautiously looked over his shoulder at the guard. "Yo' chill. What you talking about?"

"Playa, I see it all over your face. It's the same face I had before I got locked up."

"You're crazy."

"Whatever. Sinuses my ass. I done way more coke than you, so I know the drips when I see them. The only person you're fooling is yourself. You look like shit. Sniffling, eyes red, acting all paranoid."

"Hell, yeah, I'm paranoid, nigga. This is the first time I've ever been in a jail. How am I supposed to act?"

"You can't bullshit me, Eric. I've been knowing you too long."

Eric slumped in the chair, defeated. "It's that obvious?"

"Plain as day."

"I'm struggling, bruh. I really am."

"What about rehab?"

"Fuck that. I'm not an addict."

Sean rolled his eyes. "You sound like one."

"Time!" A burly guard jangled his keys.

Sean frowned. He then stood and embraced his brother. "Are you right with God?"

"I'm not sure," Eric confessed.

Sean stared at him hard. "Then ask."

Chapter Forty-three

When Eden left David Denson's office, after hearing the news, she was almost relieved. At least the agony of not knowing was over. Derek was waiting for her in the lobby and embraced her as soon as she got off the elevator. She cried on his shoulder.

"Don't worry, baby," he whispered. "It's going to be fine."

They walked hand in hand until they got to the waiting limousine outside. Eden fought back the tears. Inside the limo she broke down.

"I can't believe they fired me," she cried.

Derek gently rubbed her shoulder. "What did they tell you?"

"Th-th-they," she sobbed. "They said that while I did a great job, the ratings didn't reflect it. So they had to make a change."

A confused look crossed his face. "I've never heard of someone getting fired for doing a great job."

"Welcome to TV news," Eden said.

"Did they offer you another position?" he asked.

"Yeah," Eden said vacantly. She looked outside the window at all the people walking along Fifth Avenue. She thought about how they would find out about her being fired in the papers the next day.

"Really?" Derek was surprised. "What did they offer?"

"Overnights," she deadpanned.

"Overnights?"

"I turned them down."

"As you should have."

"They offered me something else."

"What?"

"My old job back at the local station."

"The morning show?"

Eden nodded.

"Are you going to take it?"

"Yeah, but first I want to take some time off and think about it."

"Now you're talking. Let's think about it in the Bahamas."

Eden smiled for the first time that day. "Yeah, let's."

Chapter Forty-four

"Oh my God."

Eric couldn't believe his eyes. He rubbed them to make sure he wasn't high or daydreaming. *The* one and only Halle Berry was actually sitting in his living room. She was wearing a short designer miniskirt and very little makeup. She was simply gorgeous. When she smiled at him Eric giggled like a teenager. He tried to speak but the words wouldn't come out. Halle crossed her legs, flashing just a hint of panty.

"Can I ask you a question, Eric?" she said, playfully licking her bottom lip.

Eric's heart was pounding. "You can ask me anything you want."

"Do you want to get high?" she purred.

Eric nodded yes.

"Then . . . let's . . . get . . . HIGH!" Halle growled, and

her beautiful face morphed into a monster straight out of *Night of the Living Dead.* Her voice was thunderous and demonic. She lunged at him with six-inch claws.

"Ahh!" Eric jumped awake in his bed, perspiration dripping from his forehead. His chest heaved as his eyes darted around his empty room. It was dark and silent and very hot. He rubbed the sleep from his eyes.

"Shit, I was dreaming," he muttered. "Damn, it's hot."

He got out of the bed and turned on the air conditioner. He looked at the clock. It blinked 2 AM. This was becoming a habit. He hadn't had a good night's sleep in two days, ever since he'd visited his brother in prison. The nightmares were all too frequent and rubbing his nerves raw. Either the dreams were about his dead father or some monster trying to rip him apart. Climbing back in bed, he pulled the covers up to his neck and scanned the room one last time. *Got to get some sleep.*

A few minutes later what he got was another dose of terror.

"Eric?" a low, gruff voice echoed.

"Huh? Who dat?" He jerked awake again. Once more he nervously searched his dark room. He looked at his open closet. His clothes were moving. Eric jumped out of bed and clicked on the lamp. Light flooded the room and his heart rate slowed.

"What the fuck?" he yelled. "Goddamn nightmares."

He clicked on nearly every light switch in the house. He then poured a double shot glass of Dewar's scotch. He downed the warm liquor in one gulp, saying "Ow" as his chest burned. He poured and downed another, then another.

Eric then located his coke stash and snorted big fat lines until he was sneezing white powder. High as a kite in less than three minutes, he flung open the balcony doors. Although they appeared blurry, the lights of Manhattan's famous skyline dazzled him. The stars twinkled and the breeze was cool. Eric wobbled to the waist-high railing.

"Fuck it," he slurred. "What's the use of liv . . ." His words trailed off as he took another gulp of scotch, this time swigging straight from the bottle.

He stretched his arms wide and yelled "Fuck all of ya'll" at the top of his lungs. "Sons of bitches." His voice echoed. Seconds later a "fuck you too" echoed back from an open window a few floors below. Eric staggered closer to the ledge, spitting liquor the whole way. He leaned over and stared down at the pavement, twenty-seven floors down. He stumbled, and the half-empty bottle slipped out of his hand and fell crashing onto the concrete.

"I'm next," he giggled, alcohol dribbling out of the side of his mouth.

"You took my woman," he mumbled. "My job . . . and father . . . my brother . . . What else do you want, God?" He pounded his fist against his chest. "My life?"

Eric reached up and grabbed hold of the iron railing

and struggled to pull himself up. Just when he almost had a firm grip, his hands slipped and he fell backward, crashing into a wooden deck chair. Moments later, Eric was out cold, head bleeding from a small cut, finally asleep for the night.

Chapter Forty-five

"What's his number?" LeBaron mumbled, standing just outside the nursery, admiring his new baby boy. He punched the keypad of his cell phone, so excited that he misdialed Eric's number twice. He dialed Eric's number again and after three rings, Eric picked up.

"What?" Eric said groggily.

"Wake yo' black ass up. I got something to tell you."

Silence.

"Eric?" LeBaron checked his cell phone signal. "Are you there?"

"Uh-huh."

"I just had a baby boy," LeBaron said proudly.

"Oh, great," Eric said nonchalantly. "Glad to hear it."

LeBaron made a confused face at his phone. "Did you hear what I said?"

"I heard."

"What's wrong with you?" LeBaron asked. "I just told you that my wife just gave birth."

"My father died," Eric said icily.

"Huh?" LeBaron froze.

"Pops died a few days ago."

"Pops is dead?" LeBaron sat down, stunned. He had to catch his breath. "I can't believe it. How?"

"Heart attack."

"A heart attack? Damn, E, I . . . I am so sorry. I feel terrible for you, brother."

"Thanks."

"How's your mother?"

"She's messed up, man. It was so sudden. For her to just get over dealing with the cancer and now this." Eric wanted to cry but he was all cried out.

"I'm gon' call her," LeBaron said.

"Thanks. She'll appreciate hearing from you."

"C'mon, man. Your parents are like my parents too."

"Pops always did like you. He'd always say 'Eric, you need to be more like LeBaron.' I'd tell him 'Pops, if you'd seen some of the shit LeBaron did, you wouldn't say that,'" Eric said with a sad smile.

LeBaron laughed.

"Eric, remember the time Pops went with us to Magic City? And he tried to give the stripper three quarters?"

"Pops was like, 'I'm not giving that girl a whole dollar! Just for shaking her ass. I can get your mama to do that for free.' Man, Pops was crazy."

"He was a good man, Eric."

Eric was silent.

"Eric?"

"I'm here."

"Eric, no matter what happens in our life, I am always going to be here for you. You are my brother."

"Same here, man. I really need you too. These last few months have been the hardest of my life. I've been trying really hard, LeBaron."

"Keep God first, Eric. God will never let you down."

"I know. I can honestly say that I have come to know God intimately."

"E, what can I do to help you? You want me to come to New York?"

"Nah, brother. You got a new son to look out for. Your prayers will be enough."

LeBaron looked at his sleeping son, tears in his eyes. He put his hand to the glass window. "But I will come to the funeral, okay."

"Thanks, man. That means a lot to me and the family."

"Eric?" LeBaron asked.

"Yeah?"

"I love you, brother."

"I love you too."

Chapter Forty-six

"You're so goofy," Phoenix joked while playfully elbowing LeBaron. The new father ignored her teasing. He was too busy making goo-goo eyes at their newborn son, Chase.

"Da wittle baby is so cute," LeBaron gushed. "But we still should have named you LeBaron Jr."

"Don't even joke," Phoenix deadpanned.

"What about as a nickname?" LeBaron pleaded.

"No," she said firmly.

Defeated, LeBaron kissed his son on the forehead and stroked his soft cheek with his thumb. Chase grinned and turned his mouth toward LeBaron's thumb, thinking it was a breast. Seeing how much fun LeBaron was having with the baby, Phoenix couldn't help but join in.

She kissed him on the nose. "Look at my little Chasey Wasey. You are going to be such a handsome young doctor."

LeBaron's eye arched. "A doctor? Look at the size of him. He's going to the NBA."

Phoenix waved a manicured finger. "LeBaron Brown, get those ideas out of your head. Our son is going to be a professional. Not a professional athlete."

"What if he's seven feet tall?"

She laughed. "Well, he'll be one tall doctor."

The proud parents marveled at their creation. They had brought him home a few days earlier and in that time had managed to videotape or digitally photograph Chase's every waking moment.

LeBaron slid his hand into Phoenix's and looked deep into her eyes. "I love you so much, baby."

"I love you too." She hugged him.

"Can I be honest with you?" LeBaron asked.

"Of course, baby," Phoenix said.

"Ever since you got pregnant, you've been, uh . . ." He started to stammer.

Phoenix gave him a look. "I've been what?"

"Um, a little ummm . . . dammit, you've been evil as hell."

Her look melted into a smile. "I know. I know, baby. I was a real bitch, huh?"

"I wouldn't say you were a bi—" LeBaron paused. He wasn't sure if this was a test. He then let out a hearty laugh. "Yeah, I'd have to say you were a real bitch."

Chapter Forty-seven

One of David Swift's final wishes was to be buried down home among his ancestors. He was always a country boy at heart, born and raised in the tiny backwater town of Oberlin, Louisiana. Located in Allen Parish, in the southwestern part of the state, Oberlin boasted a population of just one thousand people, the kind of town where everybody knew everything about everybody. They liked it quiet and sleepy. There were no big chain stores. Oberlinians were content with Bill's Dollar Store. You'd never find a McDonald's or Burger King there either. Danny's had the hamburger business all locked up. Race relations hadn't changed much in the town's one-hundred-year history. Whites generally stayed on their side of town and blacks stayed on theirs. Lucy's café was still segregated, by choice, that is.

Oberlin was divided by quarters. The center of the

black quarter was Mt. Calvary Baptist Church, eighty-seven years old and the place where generations of Swifts were baptized and funeralized. As usual, it was hot as a cotton field inside the small wooden church. Seemed like the congregation could never collect enough money for the building fund to purchase an air conditioner. "No matter," to quote one elderly deacon. "It's hotter in hell." Still, matronly ushers walked up and down the aisle handing out small hand fans. Mt. Calvary was packed. Two things were guaranteed to bring country folks out of the house: weddings and funerals. The two hundred or so people in the church whispered among themselves as the choir softly sang and church officials made final preparations.

Eric, his mother, Shirley, his outspoken grandmother Jessie Lee, and other family members sat stoically in the front pew. Shirley was stone-faced, a million thoughts and emotions swirling inside her mind. Eric fidgeted and kept scanning his watch. Now and again he casually looked to the back of the church, thinking, *Where is LeBaron? I hope he didn't get lost.*

Eric needed his boy for support. He had wanted to say a few words about how much his father meant to him, and as the time ticked the more nervous he became. *I have to be strong. I have to represent for Pops.*

He sat there searching the depths of his mind, trying to find the right words to pay homage to his father. Eric had promised himself that he wouldn't cry. Hearing the soft cries of grief throughout the church, it was a promise he wasn't sure he could keep. He was also awed by the grandeur of the ceremony. David was a highly decorated veteran of the Vietnam War and was entitled to full military honors. There was an honor guard platoon dispatched from the nearby base at Fort Polk to escort the body. The soldiers, all spit and polish, would also give David a twenty-one-gun salute while a lone bugler blew taps at the burial site. Eric and the other family members stared at the simple yet elegant mahogany casket draped with an American flag, each lost in their own thoughts.

"Lord," Jessie said, nudging Shirley's aunt Gloria. "Fondel's Funeral Home did a damn good job. They give you your money's worth."

"They sho' did," Gloria concurred.

Jess continued. "But me, I just want to be put in a pine box."

Moments later the Reverend Henry Eldridge III mounted the pulpit. He was elderly yet still commanded authority, the same way his father and grandfather did before him in this very spot.

Eric smiled. *He looks just like Sammy Davis Jr.*

After saying a short prayer, Reverend Eldridge addressed the congregation. "You know life is real funny. I can remember baptizing David Swift. And my daddy baptized his daddy. His family has a long history in this tiny little town. David left here a long time ago and it is an honor that he chose to come back home."

"Amen," said the church.

"If there is one thing that I can say to describe David and his family, it would be that they are good people."

"Good people," someone in the back row said.

"A short while ago, while I was in my office, a young man came and asked me if it would be alright if he stood in the pulpit while he said a few words about how much David Swift meant to him. That young man was his son." The reverend pointed to Eric. "He's sitting right there."

Eric nodded. His heart was fluttering like butterfly wings.

"You know what I told him?" Reverend Eldridge continued.

"Whatcha tell him, Rev'run'?" the head deacon said.

"I said there ain't no other place in this church for you to talk to the people but in this pulpit."

People in the church started clapping and stomping their feet.

"Come up here, son."

Eric stood and took a deep breath. He squeezed his mother's hand. She was crying. He walked the few steps to the pulpit and looked out over the congregation. A sea of expectant black and brown faces stared back at him. They seemed hungry to hear what he had to say.

Eric cleared his throat. *Stay strong, Eric. Don't cry. This is for Pops.*

"When my mama told me that my pops had died I thought I was going to die. My heart just cracked in half because I loved my daddy. I'm not ashamed to say it."

"Well," Reverend Eldridge said.

Eric's confidence started to grow. "When other kids had this football player or that superstar as their hero, I had my pops. My daddy ain't never steered me wrong. He was always there for me. He came to every football game, and he treated me the same no matter if I won or lost. Even when I was a little boy, he talked to me like a man. Now, he tore my behind up when I did wrong, but he explained to me why he had to do it."

The congregation laughed.

"Right, Mama? You know Daddy could whip some behind."

Shirley nodded her head and smiled. At that moment in the back of the church, a young man took a seat in the last pew. It was LeBaron. Eric smiled. *My man.*

"I am a grown man but I'm scared." Eric made a sweeping motion with his hand. "I'm like, what am I gon' do now that Daddy's gone? Who am I going to confide in? Who is going to give me the answers? You know what? I heard his voice. It was clear as a bell. It was during one of our last conversations. He was real sick and the chemo was really doing a job on him. He looked into my eyes and said, 'Son, I'm ready to die.' Ready to die? That crushed me. 'Not you, Pops,' I said. 'Superheroes don't die. You're my superhero. I can't go on without you.' Pops just smiled at me and said, 'Son, I will always be with you.' But he also said not to depend on him or nobody else in this world. He said depend on the Lord."

The church shouted, "Amen."

"I'm in the house of the Lord so I'm not about to lie to you. I don't go to church often." Eric paused for a few seconds. "See, right there I'm lying. I don't really go to church at all."

Even Reverend Eldridge laughed at that.

"But I have a close and personal relationship with God. And God has been talking to me lately. God's been talking to me in the sort of strange ways that will make a man listen."

Eric became silent, as if trying to summon the courage to continue.

"God is good," an elderly woman sang.

"Take your time, young man," Reverend Eldridge said.

Eric adjusted his tie and cleared his throat. "I promised myself that I wasn't gon' cry. Not 'cause I'm too tough but because I've prayed about it and God told me not to mourn but to celebrate my father's life. He had a hard upbringing but he made something out of himself. He married a good woman. She's right there. I love you, Mama."

"I love you too, son," Shirley whispered through her tears.

"And God also put something else on my mind, ya'll. We think we're the only ones who've felt the pain of a dying loved one. God knows that kind of pain very well."

"Yes, Lord" could be heard from all over the church.

"My father died. God's son died." The congregation started clapping, then stamping their feet.

Eric walked down from the pulpit and stood beside the casket. He pointed at it. "My father always took care of his family. He told me he loved me all the time. David Swift was a good man. He was the greatest man I've ever known and I'm proud to be his son. There will never be a day that he will not be a part of my thoughts. He will be a part of every breath. Every tear. Pops, with you gone the sun won't shine as bright, the sky won't seem as blue. I miss you so much already. How can mere words praise the greatest man I've ever known? And how can I question the reasons that God has called you home? I love you, Pops. Thank you." The church was silent as he walked to his seat.

"That boy sho' can preach," Jessie Lee blurted out, breaking the silence.

Eric had buried his father and he had buried the hatchet with his best friend, LeBaron. Now he felt that it was time to dig deep and bury his feelings for Eden once and for all. To do that he had to first make things right with her. He had given up all hope of ever having an intimate relationship with her, but even so, he wanted to apologize. He had to; she deserved as much. In the words of David, it was time for Eric to "tie up his loose ends."

But how was he to do it? He couldn't call her. She was definitely not trying to hear what he had to say. After rummaging through his wallet, pockets, and desk drawers, he found her business card. On it was her email address.

Suddenly, Eric was experiencing a severe case of writer's block. He stared hard at the computer screen, hoping that the words would magically spring forth. He walked to his balcony and looked at the boats sailing along the Hudson River. He popped in a CD by Sean Baker, a hot new R & B artist. Eric's favorite track was "Foolish Man," a soul-searching testament to the mistakes that men make. The hard-hitting lyrics were just the inspiration he needed. Eric closed his eyes and started typing. It was as if he was tickling the ivories of a piano, making music out of misery.

Subject: After you read this I'll never bother you again.

Dear Eden,

I've fallen fast asleep upon satin sheets. I've caressed the finest silks from foreign lands. But nothing I've ever touched or held felt as soft and tender as your hands. I've gazed upon magnificent horizons. I've been held spellbound by blue skies. But nothing prepared me for the enchantment I experienced from the magic of your eyes. I've basked in the sparkle of radiant diamonds, soaked in the brilliant rays along sun-drenched isles. But it was like a candle when compared to the bonfire of your smile. I swear I wanted to sweep you off your feet. I wanted you to feel butterflies. I wanted to ignite your deepest desires, melt your heart, and make you forget about any other guys. But I lied to you. For that I apologize.

I toyed with your emotions. I was a wolf in sheep's clothing. A thief in the night. My actions toward you proved that I was less than a real man. I apologize from the bottom of my heart. I honestly didn't know what I was getting into. You made a fool out of me. I thought that you were like most of the women I have known. I underestimated you and for that I apologize.

I hate love and I despise the fact that I love you so much. But I know that I'm doomed to a life of tortured memories of your gentle touch. Eden, I die a little inside every day we're apart. I'm unable to die completely because you have what is left of my heart. I see your face in every cloud, I smell your perfume in every breeze. I messed up a good thing. And for that I apologize. And if we ever see each other again, you don't have to say hi. But if you forgive me, I want you to just smile that beautiful smile and wink your eye.

Eric read over his letter, took a long deep breath, and clicked send.

Chapter Forty-eight

Eric sighed. *Five hundred channels and not a damn thing on.* He flipped through the channels in hopes of finding something to get his mind off his troubles and off the rest of the cocaine on the coffee table. He could swear that it was talking to him. *Come and take a sniff.*

He'd flipped through all the main stations and was looking at the local cable channels. His phone rang. It was Dirty Dre.

"Wh-wh-what's up, E?" Dirty stuttered.

"Nothing, Dirty. Just watching TV but ain't nothing on."

"You sound down."

"Dirty, you don't know the half."

"Sounds like you need a road trip."

"I need something. What's up?"

"There's this new strip club uptown."

Eric frowned. "Nah, man. I'm cool. Strip clubs are played out."

"N-n-not this one."

"How so?"

"Man, they got women from everywhere. My boy told me they got at least twenty girls in there that look like Halle Berry."

Eric laughed. "Remember the last time we heard that? The stripper had more pipe than Chuck Berry."

"Nah, man. Look, they got honeys from all over the planet. Yo, they even got g-g-girls from Hawaii."

Eric perked up. "Did you say Hawaii?"

"Yeah? You ever have sex with a Hawaiian?"

"Never!" he shot back.

"They have sex differently."

"Huh?" Eric said. "How they gon' do it differently?"

"My brother was in the army over there and he said one girl smoked a cigarette with her cat!"

"What? I'm in. Let's go," Eric said. "What time we hooking up?"

"I-I-I'm going to call you back in about an hour and give you the address. You meet me there."

Eric was excited. He resumed flipping through the channels.

At the sight of a young preacher standing in the pulpit, Eric froze. The young pastor was real animated, waving his arms in the air. Eric leaned forward and squinted.

"Oh shit! That's Reverend Francois," he said out loud. "I didn't know he had a show." Eric unmuted the remote and turned up the volume.

"The mirror casts many reflections," Reverend François said. "It reveals the true self, the one that we look at when we're all alone."

A ripple of amens flowed through the packed church. He paused for it to quiet down. "The mirror can also show the world the image that many of us spend our entire lives cultivating. It's called *the lie*."

"Yes, Lord," a deacon bellowed.

"Mankind may lie, but not the mirror. We venture forth into the world wearing a mask of lies. The mask allows us to act all tough and hard. The mask allows us to hide the ugly truth of what we are, who we are, frightened and confused human beings searching for answers and a place in the world."

"Yes, Jesus!" a choir member shouted. "God is great."

"Is that not what life is? The long search for the answers to why. Why are we here? Why must life be filled with struggle?"

"Tell us why, Preacher," someone in the back yelled.

"Life must be filled with toil in order for us to be purified when it ends. Our hearts and souls are like dirty garments that have to be scrubbed and washed. But instead of water, life uses fire. We are constantly being scorched by pain and raked across the hot coals of despair. And after evil's poison has been burned away by faith, we're rewarded with life's most precious gift, happiness. The mirror allows us to bask in the glory of our vanity, yet strips us naked and makes a mockery of the very beauty we work so hard to create. That is why we must pull off the mask and face the world on our terms, not the ones mankind dictates. There is no way to defeat the world at its own game, therefore we have to make new rules, our own rules. One should control one's destiny, never allowing another to mold and shape how and when they should act. The key to tapping into the power of self is the mastering of our emotions. Until a person can achieve this, he or she will always wear the mask and forever be a pawn."

"Preach it," came the sounds from the congregation. They were into it. Many of them were standing and shouting. The organ player was smashing on the keys, emphasizing every point the reverend was making.

"I'm tired of being a pawn," Reverend Francois said, throwing off his robe. The other preachers looked at each other. "I just took off my robe and that ain't all I'ma take off."

I know he ain't gon' take his clothes off, Eric thought in disbelief. Reverend Francois looked like he was about to have a heart attack.

"I'm 'bout to take my mask off," Reverend Francois continued. He walked down the aisle. "Ya'll want me to take it off?"

"Take it off," the congregation yelled.

Eric turned the TV off. It was too much, and besides, he had to get ready to go to the strip club with Dirty.

"The mask, huh?" he said, walking to the bathroom. "We need to take off the mask. That was real deep."

Epilogue

"Driver, stop. This is the place. Here on the right," Eric said.

The building was huge and the small parking lot was packed. As soon as Eric got out of the car he could hear music blasting from the street. It sounded like a huge party was going on inside, and he couldn't wait to get in. He marveled at the beautiful women standing outside the doors. Eric was surprised he didn't see many men around. A couple of the women smiled at him as he walked up the steps. One of them wearing a tight yellow dress handed him a piece of paper. It looked like some type of flyer. Eric smiled back, casually folded and pocketed the paper without looking at it.

The closer he got to the front door the louder the music pumped. He could feel the bass in his chest. Eric pushed open the door and the music enveloped him. He stood there for a moment soaking in the ambience. Eric let out a big smile because standing at the other end of the long aisle was Reverend Francois.

"That's right. Come to the Lord," he said to the visitors in the congregation. He noticed Eric and smiled. There was a crowd of people standing before the minister. Some were swaying and praying softly. A few of the more lively ones were jumping up and down while ushers fanned them.

Reverend Francois sang, "Is there anybody here who the Lord has made a way for?" Hundreds of hands waved in the air. "I asked is there anybody here who the Lord has made a way for?" Eric raised his hand. He felt a tingle running up his spine and his eyes were watering. Reverend Francois waved him forward. "You, brother in the back. Come," he said. "If you take one step to God, God will take two steps to you."

As Eric walked up the long aisle, people on both sides smiled welcomingly, patted him on the back, or shook his hand. The church had the feel of a family reunion. Halfway down the aisle, Eric blinked his eyes in disbelief at a beautiful yet familiar woman staring wide-eyed at him. It was Eden. She smiled and *winked her eye*. Eric nodded and kept walking. It was as if he was dreaming and floating in slow motion. His mind raced through all that had happened to him.

Life must be purified by struggle. That's what God has been trying to show me. Through pain comes love. God's love. The ultimate love. Coming to New York and getting caught up in the

*nightlife . . . alcohol . . . drugs . . . women . . . losing my job . . .
Eden . . . Pop dying. God was preparing me.*

When he made it to the altar Eric stood among a dozen
people and closed his eyes. They embraced him. The
church felt his pain.

Reverend Francois stepped down from the pulpit. He
hugged Eric.

"Out of the worst of times can come the best of times,"
he whispered to him.

Eric nodded.

Now I understand. Eric smiled, tears running down his
face. It had finally clicked. *I got seduced and took a bite out of
the Big Apple and nearly lost my shot at the real Eden.*

9 780743 483094